MORE BOOKS BY PARKER GREY

Boss Me Dirty
An Office Romance

School Me Dirty
A College Romance

Ride Me Dirty
A Cowboy Romance

Double Dirty Mountain Men
An MFM Ménage Romance

Double Dirty Royals
An MFM Ménage Romance

Rule Me Dirty

Parker Grey

Chapter One

Josephine

The car behind me is getting closer, its engine revving and then purring as I jam my fists deeper into my jacket pockets and force myself to stand up straight, eyes ahead, and *keep walking*.

Don't look scared, I remind myself, desperately trying to remember every last bit of safety advice given by my parents' security team. *Act confident, like there are people waiting for you wherever you're going.*

The engine growls again, even closer this time. I suck in a breath and quicken my pace, still forcing my spine perfectly upright even as cold sweat slides down my back, my stomach clenched in a knot. Tears are pricking at my eyeballs, no matter how hard I try to fight them back, teeth clenched.

I wish I had pepper spray. Hell, I wish I had *keys*, but I'm not even sure our doors lock. Why have locks when you have guards twenty four hours a day, seven days a week?

The car comes closer, and now I can hear the men inside it *laughing*, even though the windows are rolled up. The sound makes my blood run cold, because I know for a *fact* that they're laughing about me, or about what they're about to do to me.

I know that because there's no one else on this street, just long gray concrete buildings, the shutters down, the streetlights not even on yet, the sidewalks cracked with weeds growing between them. It's completely deserted except for me and the men in the car, and there's *nothing* I can do but keep walking.

My phone's still at home. My wallet's still at home.

Even now, I can't get my father's voice out of my head.

You're marrying him, and it's final.

I didn't think. I just *bolted*, a mixture of rage, disgust, indignation, and revulsion boiling through me. I'm lucky I was already wearing this jacket, because if I hadn't been I'd be cold right now in addition to everything else.

A car window winds down with a hum. I pick up the pace even more, now nearly running, even though I know it's not going to do me any good.

"Hey, baby," says an ugly voice, clearly more threatening than romantic. "What's a pretty girl like you doing all the way out here?"

I swallow hard and take a deep breath.

"Fuck off!" I shout over my shoulder, trying to sound as tough as I can.

It comes out a squeak, and several men all laugh. I don't *dare* turn around to see how many there are.

"Shit, girl, you won't be that feisty when you've got my dick in your mouth," the man says, and the rest laugh again.

I'm shaking, but I keep walking. I'm almost to a corner with a stop light, and I'm *praying* that the cross street saves me somehow — that there are other cars, a open business, a single person in the street, *anything.*

"Listen," the man goes on. "Get in my car now and I won't even choke you with it."

More laughter, and now my face is burning with humiliation along with everything else. I don't answer, just pretend I can't hear him as I walk up to the corner, forcing myself *not* to cry as I look both ways down the cross street.

That's when I see my salvation. It's nothing but a dimly lit doorway with a half-lit neon sign over it, but I don't *care*. Lights mean people, and people mean telephones and the police and getting home instead of dragged into a car.

Before I know what I'm doing, I *run*. My feet slap the uneven pavement and I nearly trip a couple of times, arms waving madly in the air, my heart already beating wildly, but I don't stop until I'm in front of the lit doorway, one hand on the door handle.

The car's engine roars behind me, all the men inside it laughing hysterically, like this is the funniest joke anyone's ever told. For a split second I wonder what's *behind* this door.

But then I realize I don't care, and I yank it open.

The car peels away with a shriek of tires and raucous laughter, and the smell of stale beer and tequila hits me dead in the face.

It's a bar. Just a bar, some shitty, seedy dive in the deserted, industrial part of the city. The rent's probably really cheap, and that's how they stay open.

I walk inside, letting the door slam behind me, and when it does *every* head in the place turns toward me.

I freeze. They're all men. They're mostly middle-aged, or at least they look it — every last face surly and weathered, most of them stuck in a perpetual scowl. They all *glare* at me like I've just kicked their dog, and I freeze, wondering if I've just disturbed some kind of secret meeting.

Just ask to use the phone, for fuck's sake, I think. *Call the palace, ask for a ride, and you'll be done.*

I force my breathing to slow, even though I can feel the sweat running down my neck and back, and walk calmly and confidently for the bar.

Everyone watches me. *Everyone*, the bartender included, and even when I step up he looks at me like I'm some sort of poisonous animal that's learned to talk.

"Hi," I say, as politely as possible. "Could I please use your phone to make a phone call? I forgot my phone at home."

He doesn't answer, just looks me up and down, his scowl deepening as he crosses his arms over his chest.

"You gonna buy something?" he finally asks.

Let me make a phone call and I'll fucking knight you, I think, though it seems unwise to say *that* out loud.

"I'm afraid I also forgot my wallet," I say, making myself sound as calm and collected as possible. "I promise, I'll be two minutes."

"Phone's for customers," he says, turning his back.

"You need a drink, I've got five dollars I could exchange for something else," says a wheezy, slimy voice to my right.

The hairs on the back of my neck stand up again, and I summon every ounce of self-possession I've got as I turn toward the man.

"What's a phone call worth to you?" he goes on, grinning. He's missing half the teeth in his mouth.

"You look like you ain't even had the bloom taken off your rose yet, and you *sure* do seem like you're in a hell of a pickle, little girl."

"I'm not fucking anyone for a phone call," I say, my voice as cold as I can make it.

The man just laughs, the bartender's back still turned, and out of nowhere he grabs my wrist with surprising strength, so hard that I *yelp*.

"You sure about that?" he grins.

"Let me *go*," I say through gritted teeth, tears springing to my eyes as his wire-like fingers *dig* into my wrist.

He just laughs again.

"I *really* think you should trade with—"

The man goes silent, his smile fading as he looks over my head, and suddenly I realize there's someone there.

Someone *looming* over both of us. Someone who's made this jerk and every other jerk and this stupid bar suddenly go quiet.

"She *said,* let her go," a voice rumbles, deep and husky and *powerful*. It sends chills down my spine.

The guy lets me go, and I yank my wrist away,

flexing and shaking out my fingers.

"You got a *problem*?" Half-Toothless says, slowly standing up from his bar stool. "'Cause I don't see how this is none of *your* business."

He wavers a little on his feet, and I back away from the two of them, because the *last* thing I want is to get into the middle of a bar fight right now.

And when I turn, I see my defender for the first time.

The bar's barely lit, but I don't need light to see that he's *easily* six and a half feet tall, muscles practically bulging out of a well-worn black leather jacket. He flexes one huge, scarred hand as I watch, the ropey muscles of his jaw working as he does.

He's *hot*. Even now, with all my fight-or-flight instincts blaring, I can take one second and appreciate that my savior is six-plus feet of pure muscle with golden-brown hair and the kind of jawline you see in ads for fancy watches.

Drool-worthy. Any other time, I'd be scraping my jaw off the floor, but right now, I glance back at Half-Toothless.

"It's my business now," Leather Jacket says.

"Now, either you leave or we can *discuss* it."

The drunk with not enough teeth stands there for a moment. He's breathing heavily, almost snorting like a bull, and he thinks about this for a *long* time.

Then he goes to punch Leather Jacket, and he takes so long to wind up that even *I* can tell what's happening.

It's over in a flash. The punch goes wide, and Leather Jacket barely moves as he catches the other man's fist in his own massive hand, jerks him around, and twists his arm behind his back until Half Toothless *screams*.

I clap my hands to my mouth and gasp, just as Leather Jacket glances over at me, his gaze inscrutable.

He lets Toothless go, and the other man just crumples to the floor without moving.

Leather Jacket glances around the bar calmly. Everyone else turns back to their drinks, and the bartender acts like nothing at all happened, as Jacket grabs his glass, tosses its contents back, then puts it back on the bar with a heavy *thunk*.

Does this mean I can use the phone now? I

wonder, but then Leather Jacket turns toward me. He steps over the crumpled form in the middle of the bar and comes up to me, holding something out in one hand.

I'm not looking at that. I'm looking at his face.

I could only see half of it before, but now I can see all of it.

He's still handsome, almost cartoonishly handsome, but I'm not staring at that either.

I'm staring at the scar, a thick line that runs from his hairline, over one eye, to his chin. I have no idea how you *get* a scar like that, but it can't be good.

"Hey," he says, his voice gruff.

Fear stabs through my heart one more time, and I look down frantically at his extended hand.

"I thought you wanted to make a phone call," he says.

Chapter Two

Leo

She exhales, her shoulder slumping in relief, as she reaches out to take my phone in her small, delicate hand.

"Thanks," she says, her voice quiet and whispery.

She clears her throat and stands up straighter, like she's trying not to look scared.

"Sorry about all this," she says, sounding a little stronger. "I didn't—"

She breaks off, then shakes her head like she's trying to clear it.

"I didn't think at all," she says, dialing a number. "It's a long story."

She holds the phone up to her ear, her eyes still on mine, and I turn away because I can't look at her any more.

11

Princess Josephine is even more beautiful than she is in her pictures. Even here, in this dark, seedy bar she radiates innocence, vulnerability, and something *else*.

Something that calls to the darkest part of me. The part I'd hoped to bury.

Something that screams *take me*.

Ruin me.

Make me yours.

I don't know what the hell she's doing here, but thank fucking God she showed up at the dark hole I picked to hide in.

And thank God that she didn't recognize me, or there's a good chance she'd have run screaming back into the street.

I scan the dive again while she talks, just to make sure no one else is thinking of trying anything.

The guy with half his teeth is slowly pushing himself off the floor, giving me sulky glares, but he just gets back on his barstool and orders another drink without making a fuss.

Everyone else pretends like nothing happened, like they weren't all just fucking complicit. Like they didn't each just watch this girl get denied a simple *phone call*, for fuck's sake.

They're a bunch of worthless goddamn animals, I think. *They're not even fit to be called human.*

If these were the old days, and we were in Szegravia, I could *do* something about it. Toss them all in the mines and never think about it again, but not now. Now we've got *trials* and *burden of proof* and *defense lawyers*, and even if those things are usually good, sometimes I want to throw them all out the window and go back to *a hand for a hand*.

"Okay, thanks," says behind me. "See you soon."

I turn, and she hands my phone back. I slide it into my pocket just as her eyes dart to the scar and then away again, still with no glimmer of recognition.

Good. I prefer it that way. She'll know what I am soon enough.

"Someone's coming to pick me up," she says, handing my phone back, her huge blue eyes meeting mine. I can tell she's trying to sound and act brave, like she's not scared, but it's not working.

Every cell in my body is screaming *protect her*, even though I know the one person she *truly* needs protecting from is me.

"I'll walk you out," I say, sliding my phone back into my pocket.

"You don't have—"

"I'm going to walk you out."

Her eyes flash, and her perfect lips just *barely* part, like she's about to refuse and fight back. But then she glances at the bartender and at the front door, and she acquiesces.

"Thanks," she says, and lowers her eyes.

In a split second I'm unbearably hard, my dick aching so bad I think I might blow a blood vessel. I was halfway there already, just *looking* at her perfect body, the swell of her breasts, imagining her plush lips as she cries out.

But *this* is it, fucking incredible, the stuff wet dreams are made of. Princess Josephine *submitting*, even to being walked outside, makes me crave her submission in every *other* way imaginable.

I want her on her knees, hands tied behind her back, my cock parting her lips.

I want her legs spread while she gasps and I tease her to the edge of orgasm with my tongue, over and over again, refusing to give her satisfaction until I decree it.

I want her *trembling* as she comes for the fifth time in a row, my cock deep inside her drawing out climax after climax.

In the darkness, I just smile and play the part of *rescuing gentleman.*

"Ladies first," I say, and gesture toward the door.

Josephine walks through, and I watch her ass as she does, a perfect bubble swaying from side to side. If I weren't already rock hard I would be *now*.

Outside, the streetlights have just come on, but they only make the deserted street look even more abandoned. Far away, a car drives and then turns. The stoplight turns from green to yellow to red, then back to green.

There's *no one* out here but us. I've got no idea why this shitty bar is here. I just know I found it when I was looking for a place to hide, because darkness is my friend.

"Looks like we've got a little time," I say, hands firmly in my pockets, dick *throbbing* against my jeans. "What's a nice girl like you doing down here with no phone and no wallet?"

She sighs again, then pushes a hand through her blond hair, a far away look in her eyes.

"It was dumb," she admits. "I sort of... spazzed and ran out my front door without thinking, wandered for a while without looking where I was going, and next thing I know I'm down here at night like an idiot."

"What made you spaz?" I ask.

She clears her throat and looks uncertain, running the tip of her tongue along her top lip, like she's thinking.

"My parents... gave me some bad news," she says. "And I really, really needed to leave and clear my head."

Something clenches in my stomach.

Bad news.

"What kind of bad news?" I press.

A car pulls up to the stoplight on the cross street, and waits. We both crane our necks to see it.

Our light goes red. The car makes a left turn and starts gliding down the street toward us, a black Town Car.

It's *obviously* Princess Josephine's ride, and she blushes. She still doesn't realize I know who she is.

"Just... bad news, I don't really want to go into it," she says, forcing herself to sound cheerful. "That's my ride. Thanks so much for letting me use your phone and waiting with me."

"I'm happy to help," I say, the manners my mother drilled into me coming out. "Try not to wander bad neighborhoods at night any more."

The car pulls up and stops. She waves to the driver, and I walk forward, opening the back door for her.

"I'll try," she says, then pauses. "Listen, is there anything I can do for you? I'm so sorry, I didn't think to ask—"

I just chuckle.

"Not a single thing," I say.

She frowns, but sits in the car. I close the door after her, and she waves to me once before the car pulls away.

Bad news, I think.

I'm pretty sure I know what the bad news her parents gave her was.

And I'm pretty sure it's *me*.

Chapter Three

Josephine

"Hold *still*," Katarina admonishes me.

"It *tickles*."

"Then stop being ticklish," she says.

I clench my teeth together, and she keeps lightly brushing powder onto my face.

"I'm almost done," she says, giving my cheekbones a few more swipes as her enormous belly brushes against me.

Katarina steps back and admires her handiwork.

"There," she says. "You look *almost* human."

"Maybe we're going the wrong direction with this," I say, giving myself a once-over in the mirror. "Maybe I should look like a swamp monster so Prince Leo takes one look and runs right back to Szegravia."

Katarina just rolls her eyes.

"You're overreacting," she says. "Give the poor guy a chance. He's been cooped up in that castle for *years*, the least you can do is be nice, Jo."

"There's a *reason* he's been in the castle for years," I mutter.

"No, there's a *rumor*," Katarina says firmly. "Remember when you were allegedly snorting a combination of cocaine and industrial cleaner off a stripper's ass in Moscow last year?"

I wasn't, *obviously*, but it didn't stop the tabloids from reporting it.

"That was different."

"That was *also* a rumor."

"I think it's romantic," sighs Florentina, from her chair behind us.

She's been quiet most of this time, half listening to us and half staring off into space, day dreaming. It's kind of her *thing*.

Katarina and I both just look at her and wait.

"You know, the prince locked away in the tower, some kind of tortured soul, and he can only *truly* be understood by his one love?"

She sighs dramatically. Katarina and I look at her, then at each other.

"Or, he's a perfectly nice guy with a very shitty public relations team, and he picked the wrong way to deal with infamy at a young age," Katarina says.

"I hope you're right," I say.

She grabs a sapphire blue gown on a hanger, unzips it, and bunches it all together so it's just fabric around a hole.

"Arms up," she orders. "Florrie, come make sure the dress doesn't screw up her hair, will you?"

Between the two of them, they maneuver the gown over my hair and makeup, and Florentina zips it up my back as I check myself out in the mirror.

I've gotta give it to them, because I look *good*. You can't even tell that I spent an hour crying this morning.

"You sure do clean up nice," Katarina says, and pats my butt.

I make a face at her, but for an instant I think of the guy who saved my ass at the bar last night. Despite everything that's about to happen, I keep *thinking* about him.

His eyes, deep brown and almost *feral*. The way he barely smiled at me.

His muscles. Good Lord, his *muscles*.

And I didn't even get his name. Of all the dumb things I did yesterday, that was probably the dumbest.

"Go get 'em tiger," Katarina says, and the three of us leave my dressing room.

• • •

In the throne room, I feel like I'm having an out of body experience. Like *I'm* actually somewhere else, just watching Princess Josephine of Tomassia sit behind her parents, smiling prettily, greeting foreign dignitaries one by one.

Every time the massive door to the throne room opens again, my heart leaps into my throat, pins and needles prickling along my skin as I think, *is that him? Is **that** him?*

I'm supposed to marry the man, and I don't even know what he looks like. *No one* does, except his family and servants.

There are no pictures of Prince Leo. Rumor has it that he hasn't left his castle in almost fifteen years, not since *the incident*. That's how the tabloids and the newspapers always talk about it.

The incident.

But there are rumors that he's an enormous, *brutish* beast of a man, and that he's so ugly that mirrors crack when he walks by. I've heard that he only speaks in grunts and growls, and that once when he got angry, he threw a table out a window.

And I'm supposed to *marry* him.

My parents just rolled their eyes at the rumors, of course, because according to them he's perfectly nice, just shy.

But there's shy, and then there's *beastly*.

The Duke and Duchess of Canterview bow once more, then move off to the side, sitting in the gallery. Every head turns toward the huge doors at the end of the hall, and yet again, my stomach clenches.

They open, and then, for a long moment, nothing happens. The darkness beyond them yawns, the space deep and empty, and my heart *seizes* in my chest.

It's him. It has to be him.

Anyone else would just walk in like a normal person.

Suddenly, a man strides into the room. Even from the other side of the room I can tell that he's huge, tall and wide and *built*, and there's something wild and untamed about him, despite the perfectly tailored suit he's wearing.

And he's *powerful*, walking in like he owns this room and this castle and this whole country, an aura of pure *domination* surrounding him.

No one has to tell me who he is. Just from the reaction he gets, all the nobles and royals in the room going silent at once, I *know*.

It's Prince Leo. The man my parents want me to marry. Anxiety stabs through my chest, and I feel dizzy, like I can't breathe.

Not him, I think. *Anyone but him, please.*

At the dais, the man kneels, head bent, in front of my parents, the King and Queen.

"Your majesties," he says.

Something about his voice suddenly jars my breath loose, and I exhale in a rush because I *recognize* his voice from somewhere, but I can't remember where. He's familiar but he *can't* be familiar, he's a weirdo who hasn't left his castle in years and year.

I feel like the world is tilting and I'm trying to grab onto something familiar.

Think, Josephine, I order myself, but my brain freezes.

"Prince Leopold of Szegravia, please rise," my father says, his voice perfectly formal.

The man stands, lifting his head.

The second I see his face, I gasp out loud. This terrifying, feral, *beast* of a man has a scar running the length of his face, from his hairline to his jaw.

Prince Leo was my rescuer last night, and now he's staring *right* at me.

Chapter Four

Leo

I can't take my eyes off of her. I know I'm talking, saying all the correct, polite things that a well-bred prince ought to say in a foreign court, but I don't have the first fucking clue what any of it is.

All I can see is *her*, sitting a few paces behind her parents, the sapphire blue gown hugging her perfect curves. She's breathing quickly, like she's nervous, and with every breath her chest swells in *exactly* the right way to make me achingly hard.

But that's not all. It's also the look in her eyes, the way her lips parted just a little when she realized who I was.

Princess Josephine is frightened of me. That's no surprise. I've got a reputation that precedes me by miles, and even if the vicious rumors aren't true, she

26

probably *should* be frightened of me.

After all, I'm not gentle. I'm not kind. I'm sure I'm not the prince charming she's always dreamed of.

But I know that *look*. Behind the fear and the nervousness, there's something deep and wild in her eyes, in the way her lips part when she looks at me. Something that makes me *crave* her the way a drowning man craves air.

I knew it the second I saw her picture, the second I watched her on the television, a bridesmaid in her sister's unconventional wedding. It's why I'm here right now.

I sit in the throne room for a fucking *eternity*. I absolutely hate this shit, and I refuse to do it in my own court. The only reason I'm doing it *now* is because of her.

When the reception is finally over, the King, Queen, and Princesses all proceed out, Josephine giving me one last glance before she leaves.

Before I can even rise in my own seat, there's an attendant at my side, waiting to be noticed. He clears his throat politely.

"What do you—"

I force myself to stop, take a breath, and start over.

"Yes?" I ask.

His face is perfectly blank, like I didn't just growl at him.

"The royal family has requested your presence in their private sitting room," he says. "If Your Highness would follow me..."

I stand, remembering to smooth down my suit. I fucking hate wearing this thing, even if it makes me look civilized and maybe even *good*. But when I've got it on, I feel like a fake, because I'm *not* civilized unless I have to be.

We walk out of the throne room, through a few doorways and another hall, and then he pushes another door open and nods me through.

Inside are the King, the Queen, and Princess Josephine.

After a second I remember my manners and bow.

"Prince Leopold," the King says, strict and jovial all at once. "Many thanks for making the long journey to Tomassia."

He's just being polite. It was a plane flight.

I nod slightly.

"It was nothing," I say.

Princess Josephine doesn't say anything, but she's standing tall, shoulders squared and back straight, the same way she stood at the bar. The way she stands when she's trying not to look afraid.

"The Princess has offered to show you to your chambers," he goes on. "I hope you'll find them adequate."

"I'm sure I will," I say.

Josephine looks at her parents. They look back, and then after a moment, she steps forward.

"Shall we?" she asks, her voice soft but steely as she walks toward me.

She stops a few feet away, her eyes burning into mine. It's all I can do not to take her by the waist right there and *devour* her perfect, beautiful mouth with mine.

"It would be my *pleasure*," I say.

• • •

The halls are filled with servants, courtiers,

nobles, and dozens of other people rushing around to prepare for the banquet dinner tonight. Josephine and I talk stiffly, as she points out the portraits of this or that ancestor, architectural details, historical notes on the castle.

I answer in grunts and single words, because even though I'm trying to do better, just being *near* her reduces me to my basest state. All I can think about is *tearing* her dress off, pulling her hair, and taking her again and again while she whimpers, *begging* me for more.

At last, we enter the South Wing of the castle, and she leads me down a stone hallway. For once, there's no one else here, and we come up to a doorway.

"These will be your chambers," she says, turning her crystal-blue gaze on me as she stops, clearly expecting me to go in.

I don't. Instead I let my eyes roam over her body, savoring every goddamn inch of her and letting her know *exactly* what I'm doing.

I'm hard as fucking iron, and my trousers can't even begin to hide my massive erection.

I'm a *beast* in more ways than one.

"You can drop the act," I growl.

She swallows hard, but she doesn't budge an inch, just lifts her head up a little, her chin jutting out.

"What act?"

I step forward so that now we're closer. I *tower* over her by at least a foot, and maybe more, but she doesn't back down.

"The act that I didn't rescue you from the wolves last night," I say, my voice low and gravelly.

She looks down, turning her head slightly, and the cords in her neck pop. I grit my teeth together and force myself not to bite them.

"Thank you for that," she says, her voice polite and rigid. "And thank you for not telling my parents the trouble that I nearly got myself into, but—"

"But *nothing*, Princess," I say, and take another step closer.

This time she takes a step back, against the wall.

"You were running from bad news, and the bad news was *me*," I go on.

She looks me in the eye, half defiant and half nervous, and I put one hand on the wall, next to her head.

"That's not exactly what I meant," she says bravely, and I just laugh.

"You can't lie to me," I say, and now my face is just inches from hers. "You think I don't know the rumors? You think I don't know what people say?"

She swallows hard, her eyes darting back and forth.

"You think I don't know about *this*?" I ask, running one finger the length of my thick, ugly scar.

"I didn't say that," she whispers.

"I came here for one reason, princess," I growl. It's taking *everything* I have not to crush her mouth with mine right now, tear off her dress and show her *just* how uncivilized I am, but I don't.

Not yet.

"I came here to make you *mine*," I say. "Not because my parents arranged a marriage. Not because your parents requested that I marry you. I will *have* you, Princess."

Chapter Five

Josephine

I bite my lips together, a flush creeping onto my cheeks.

Take me! I want to scream, because I don't know how or why, but there's something about Prince Leo that turns my body to jelly.

But I gather every ounce of wits I have, and even though my entire body is heated beyond recognition, my core aching and hot, I open my mouth.

"That's not up to you," I whisper.

His face doesn't change at all, but I swear there's a fierce, wild light that comes into his eyes, a light that sparks something deep and *needy* inside me.

"Don't lie to yourself, Princess," he says, his voice practically dripping with danger and sex. "I can tell what you want, even from here."

He tilts his head forward, until his lips are nearly on my ear.

"And I promise to give it to you until you *scream* my name," he says, his voice vibrating through my entire being, sending shivers down my spine.

I'm holding my breath, eyes shut tight. He's right and I *hate* that he's right.

Suddenly he takes a step back, the spell broken, and he straightens his suit.

"I'll see you at dinner, then?" he asks, one hand on the doorknob.

I open my mouth. I close it. My whole body is a riot of *want* and *need* and desire and revulsion, so it takes me a moment to find the right words.

"Yes," I finally say. "Yes, of course."

He gives me one more long look up and down, then pushes his door open.

"It'll be my pleasure," he says, and then enters his chambers.

I turn on my heel and walk as fast as I possibly can without running toward my own rooms.

• • •

I shut my door and lock it, breathing hard, and lean back against it.

What just happened?! I think, frantically.

Prince Leo — beastly, unseen, uncivilized — is the man from last night. The man who stepped in and rescued me, the man who protected me, the man who graciously let me use his phone.

The man I couldn't stop *thinking* about last night, the way his shoulders filled out his leather jacket, the way his hand was rough as he gave me his phone.

And I don't know *what* happened just now. It was completely uncalled for, rude, arrogant — not to *mention* it's a total breach of etiquette to pin a princess against a wall and tell her that she's *yours*.

But now my heart's beating wildly, my whole body tingling and surging with pure, unfiltered *want*. If he'd gone on, if he'd kissed me, yanked the top of my dress down and rolled my nipples roughly between his fingers, if he'd pulled off my skirt and ripped away my thong —

"Quit it," I say out loud, even though there's no one in my room but me, and I walk away from the door and start pacing back and forth, trying not to think about what just happened.

Or how much I wanted *more* to happen.

I don't even know *what* I wanted to happen. I've never done more than kiss a boy before, my *very* strict parents have seen to that.

I mean, I'm not an idiot. I know *about* sex and how it works. I've just never done it. Or even been within miles of doing it.

I sit on my bed, hands planted at my sides, and make myself take deep breaths.

This is normal, I say. *It's... hormones or something, I don't know, you're just really worked up because something like that has never happened to you before.*

I know it's not hormones. I'm twenty-three, not sixteen. And I also know it's not because I've never gotten laid. I've had crushes before, and I've definitely had sexy thoughts about men before, but not like *this*.

This was all-consuming, totally enthralling. Like every nerve in my body was lit on fire at once.

Gently, so I don't mess up my hair, I lie back on my bed and pull the skirt of my gown up, the material slithering up my legs and to my hips.

Just don't think about Prince Leo, I tell myself. *Take care of things, just don't think about him.*

When I slide my hand under my thong, it's *soaking* wet, my lips swollen and aching with desire. Quickly, I run two fingers along my seam, shuddering as I do — *Prince Leo's tongue darting between my lips as his hands — NO, stop it!* — and start circling my clit.

God, it feels good. Better than it has in ages, because I'm so *ready* for this. I bit my lip and turn my head to one side, clutching my sheets in my left hand.

Not him, I think. *Not him. Think about the cute gardener or something.*

I try. I think about the cute gardener, taking off his shirt in the shed behind the castle... and then when he turns, he's got Prince Leo's face.

A bolt of pleasure shudders through me.

Dammit.

I rub myself faster and faster, desperate for release. Now I'm panting for breath, gasping for air, desperately trying not to think about anything but it's not working.

Prince Leo, pushing me against a wall, his hands so tight on my hips it might bruise.

Prince Leo, one hand in my hair, pulling my head back roughly as he *growls*.

Prince Leo, spinning me around and bending me over the bed, one hand holding me there as he teases me, parting my lips with the impossibly thick head of his cock, as he pushes harder and enters my tight, virgin pussy for the first—

I come. I come so hard that I cry out, fingers clutching at the bedsheets, toes curling. Even though I've gotten myself off *hundreds* of times, I come harder than I ever have before, so hard it *surprises* me.

I just lie there, letting the waves roll over me, until I can finally think and move again, and I sit up, pushing my dress back down, still a little shaky.

It's okay, I tell myself. *People fantasize about things they don't really want all the time.*

Right?

I stand, then walk slowly to my bathroom to wash my scent off of my hands before I go have dinner with the man my parents want me to marry.

Chapter Six

Leo

At the banquet, Josephine and I have been seated at different tables. I seriously consider simply sitting at her table anyway, and letting whoever's seat I take find another goddamn place to sit, but I don't.

I can act like I belong in polite company, even if I know I don't.

Besides, it's for the best. Being close to Josephine is too almost overwhelming, too much for me to take. Ever since I first saw those *awful* tabloid photos of her a few months ago, I knew she was beautiful, stunning, *luscious* in ways I don't have words for.

But being *near* her, in person, is almost more than I can take, and I don't want the animal inside me to take over in the middle of this banquet.

Dinner finishes. Afterward there's brandy and

cigars, and I force myself to partake in both, along with an incredibly tedious conversation about the economic implications of the new trade agreement between Finland and Russia.

I don't care about the trade agreement. What I *want* to do is race off to Josephine's chambers, break down the door, take her trembling body in my arms, and *taste* her.

But I want more than that from her. I can't explain it, but I need her ways I've never felt before, in ways that go beyond a single night or two.

I want to make her mine *forever*, and I know that if she thinks I'm a monster, that won't happen.

• • •

It's late before I finally get back to my chambers in the south wing of the palace, and I'm fucking exhausted from being in polite company for hours, because I know what everyone's thinking behind their smiles.

They think I'm a freak. A monster. A brute who's totally unfit to be in public, let *alone* polite society.

And I know that, despite everything, they think I'm a murderer.

This is why I haven't gone out into public in years, at least not as Prince Leopold. I've left the palace, of course; I'm not a hermit or a shut-in, and you'd be amazed at what a hat and sunglasses can do. If anything, not *officially* leaving the palace in the fifteen years or so since *the incident* has given me a more normal life than I'd have otherwise.

I walk over to the windows and look out at the moonlit gardens, intersected by neat paths, orderly like everything else in this tiny country. I watch them for a long time, because there's something soothing in their perfect layout, every corner ninety degrees, every walkway perfectly parallel.

Something moves in the corner of my vision, and I look down.

It's a woman, wearing a long dress, and she's slowly strolling along one of the paths, absentmindedly flicking flowers as she walks past them. Even though I can't see her face from my window, there's something about the way she moves, something incredibly *alluring* about the shape of her body.

I know exactly who she is.

And she *knows* that she's strolling right in front of my windows.

I lean forward slightly, gripping the stone window frame with both hands in a desperate effort to maintain control because just the sight of her *floods* me with desperate need. All I can think about is earlier today, her back against the wall.

The way her lips parted, just *barely*. The flush that rose to her cheeks, the way her back arched against the stone.

The faint, *faint* scent of arousal so strong she couldn't hide it.

And God, more than everything else, her *submission*. We both knew that she could have screamed and the guards would have come running, but she didn't. There were a million ways for her to get rid of me, but she didn't do any of them.

I'm hard again, so hard it hurts.

I know what she wants. I've *known* what she wants from the second I laid eyes on her in that bar.

And I know why she's *casually* strolling

underneath my window at midnight.

I find the nearest staircase and head down to the ground floor, then outside, into the gardens. I know I'm in full view of half the castle, but I don't give a shit if anyone sees me.

Everyone knows what I'm here for. Let them watch.

After a few minutes, I see a figure ahead of me, on the path, the dress shining dully in the moonlight, her slim waist curving out to perfect hips and an ass *made* for grabbing. I reach out and snap a flower from a rose bush.

See? I can be a fucking gentleman.

As I approach, Princes Josephine turns. She doesn't exactly look *surprised*, but she looks like she's suddenly uncertain about this.

"Your Highness," I say, and bow, presenting the flower.

"Prince Leopold," she says.

She takes the rose gingerly, like she thinks it might bite her, and her gaze lingers on the torn stem at the bottom where I pulled it from the bush.

"Call me Leo," I tell her.

"What are you doing out here, Leo?" she asks softly, though the look in her eyes tells me that she already knows.

"I should ask you the same thing," I say, stepping closer.

She glances at the wall of windows, all dark and half-hidden.

"Taking a walk," she says.

"Taking a walk below my window late at night?" I growl, stepping closer again. "There are a thousand places to walk at the palace, Princess, and you picked this one."

Josephine takes a deep breath.

"I can walk wherever I like," she says.

"And you *like* walking where I can see you," I say, stepping forward again. Now we're inches from each other, and if she can't see the enormous bulge in my pants, she's blind.

I feel like every nerve is my body is twitching, ready to jump through my skin with tension because I want to claim her mouth, push her to the ground and *ravish* her tight virgin cunt. I want to be the first man she feels there, and I want it *now*, here.

"Tell me, Princess," I whisper, sliding one hand through her hair, then locking it in place. "Are you still as wet for me as you were this afternoon?"

I pull her hair *just* slightly, and her head tilts back a fraction of an inch. She swallows, her eyelids lowering a little, her breath quickening.

"How did you know?" she asks.

I slide my other arm around her waist, my fingers digging into her back, and I grin as I tower over her.

"Lucky guess," I say.

Then I bend down, crushing my mouth with hers, and I *claim* her.

Chapter Seven

Josephine

Leo's lips are hard against my own, soft and rough all at once as he kisses me so hard I think he might leave bruises.

After a long moment he pulls back slightly, *just* enough to let me breathe, and then he *devours* me again as he pulls me against his body, his tongue pushing my lips open and tangling with my own, and I can't help but moan into his mouth.

He *growls* in response, his hand cupping my ass and dragging me against him and the absolutely *massive* lump in his pants, pressing urgently into my belly.

He must be wearing padded underwear or something, because it can't *possibly* be that big.

Leo pulls away again. My lips feel swollen and

bruised, and he's still got one hand locked in my hair, my head tilted backward, but every cell in my stupid, traitorous body is absolutely *writhing* with anticipation.

As soon as his lips leave mine, they're traveling along my jaw, to my neck, my ear, kissing and sucking and biting the sensitive skin there as I think I might lose my mind. I've got both my hands on his shoulders, but that's just for show because I'm locked tight in his arms, and it's obvious there's no way he's letting me go.

"Is this how you wanted your walk to end?" he murmurs into my ear as he finally takes his hand out of my hair and runs it down my back, grabbing my ass with both hands.

I don't answer, because it *is*, and I close my eyes again as he squeezes me hard, his erection hard against my belly.

"Or were you hoping for more?" he growls. "Maybe you wanted to end your walk with my face between your legs, licking you until you came?"

His hand moves down, sliding between my buttocks, and I gasp when he slides it between my legs, stretching the fabric of my dress.

"Or maybe you wanted me to finger-fuck your sweet little pussy while you moaned," he goes on.

Leo starts stroking me, through my skirt and panties, and it's all I can do not to whimper with pleasure.

Then he leans in, lips against my ear.

"Or maybe you were hoping your walk would end with my thick cock buried in your tight little virgin cunt," he whispers, and I *gasp*.

No one's ever talked to me this way. No one's ever even come *close*, but even though my face is burning, heat is *flooding* downward through my body with every filthy word he says.

I swallow.

"How do you know I'm a — you know..."

"*Everyone* knows you're totally untouched," he growls, his fingers still stroking me, every movement sending a shudder through my body. "It wouldn't do for a princess to be *anything* but a virgin on her wedding night."

I bite my lip as he keeps stroking me, because right now, that's the *last* thing I want. As much as I *know* I shouldn't be here, letting Prince Leo *touch* me like this, *talking* to me like this, I'm putty in his hands.

Suddenly, I hear voices coming down the path.

I gasp and try to leap away from Leo, but he doesn't let me go, just keeps stroking me through my dress and panties, his fingers more and more insistent as he chuckles.

"Stop," I whisper. "Someone's coming."

"They won't be the only one."

I blink at him for a few seconds, and *then* I understand the entendre and I blush even harder. The voices get closer, and I can tell that they're just around a bend in the path, but Leo *still* doesn't stop, his finger surprisingly rough but still milking pleasure out of me, even here, *now*.

"Leo," I whimper.

He finally stops, and then in a split second he's grabbed me by the hand, nearly pulling me off my feet, and he's pulling me through a gap in some bushes, holding the thorns back while I pass through just as the voices get louder, clearer, and I can finally hear what they're saying.

"I think it's quite a fascinating proposition," one says, and I hold my breath.

It's Count von Messer, one of my father's closest advisors.

"Fascinating, yes, but it might also be unwise," cautions another voice, this one belonging to the Earl of Strathem, another of my father's right-hand men.

Leo and I are in a small grassy area between two rows of bushes, and we're out of sight but we're not exactly *hidden*. If we do anything or make any noise, they'll hear us for sure, and they're walking with *excruciating* slowness.

"I think if the right provisions were made in the tariff, then we could..."

Leo stands behind me, his hands on my shoulders, and he bites my ear.

I gasp as a thrill runs through my body, nipples stiffening instantly.

The conversation beyond the bushes stops for a moment.

"Did you hear something?" the Count asks.

"There are stray cats who wander the gardens at night," the Earl says, dismissively. "As I was saying..."

Leo's tongue runs along the shell of my ear, and I bite my lip, forcing myself not to make any noise as his hand slithers down my body, over one hard nipple, and to the place where my hip meets my thigh.

"Better stay still and not make any noise," he growls, his voice barely registering.

I could leave. I *know* I could leave. He's not even holding me, I'm here completely of my own volition, letting this wild man touch me however he wants.

Hell, I don't even have to leave. I just have to *scream* and this is over, but I don't. I lean my head back against his thick, strong shoulder and *sigh* as he pulls the long skirt of my gown up to my waist, then slides his hand between my legs.

My legs turn to jelly almost instantly, and Leo has to wrap his arm around my chest to keep me upright as his thick, rough fingers part my lower lips roughly, slick and dripping with my juices. He strokes me slowly, barely touching me, *teasing* me.

I think my father's advisors have stopped walking and are just *standing* beyond the hedge. They haven't moved in long, long seconds, simply debating some point of economics.

"That could encourage trade, but might encourage industry to move..."

"Most of our neighboring nations have similar provisions in place..."

Leo's fingers swipe along my drooling seam and then *finally* find the sensitive button of my clit. My whole body jolts as he does, though I manage not to make any noise as he does it again and again, teasing me for a few moments, then stopping.

I'm fully leaning back against his hard, thick body. It's taking everything I have not to moan out loud, whimper, or sigh, because even though this is risky and *dangerous*, I've never wanted anything more.

Slowly, he circles my clit faster and faster, his fingers moving harder and harder. I'm in the throes of reverie, toes curling in my shoes. I can barely stay upright, and I'm arching my back against him, his thick, rock-hard erection pressing urgently between my buttocks.

He's completely and utterly in control, so in

control that he doesn't even have to keep me there physically.

And I *like* it. I like it and I want *more*, I want him to push me to my hands and knees right now, grab my hair, and plunge himself into me hard and deep and with no mercy.

I want it so bad I can feel my juices running down the inside of my leg and my breath hitches in my throat.

"Come quietly," Leo whispers, his voice so low I think I might be imagining it. "Like a good girl."

His fingers slide over my clit one more time, and that's all it takes for the pleasure to break over me like a waterfall, rivulets of pleasure running through my body, on the inside of my skin, as every muscle jolts and jerks again and again.

He doesn't stop until I'm completely finished, gasping for breath, my body trembling against him, his arm still holding me tight. Leo keeps stroking me softly after I've come, dipping his fingers between my soaked lips, and even though I *just* finished I desperately want him to push inside me, stroke my sensitive inner wall while I moan.

"I disagree that the wider economic landscape would be so affected..." I hear the Earl say, and swallow hard.

I'd nearly forgotten that they were there, and that I can't *imagine* what would happen if my ultra-strict father's two closest advisors found his middle daughter in the bushes with *Prince Leo* of all people, her dress around her hips.

"Frankly, the only way to know what would happen is..." the Count answers, his voice fainter.

I don't move, even though Leo keeps stroking me, teasing me, *almost* sliding his fingers into my tight entrance but then moving away. Slowly, I hear their footsteps move off, and finally, Leo stops, taking his hand out of my panties.

"Do you like it when I make you come?" he growls, and I turn my head.

He licks his fingers off, one by one, locking eyes with me as he does.

Chapter Eight

Leo

Princess Josephine is fucking *delicious*. I've thought a thousand times about tasting her sweet nectar, about licking and tongue-fucking her until she came, but it's even better than I thought it could be.

Fuck, I didn't even eat her out. I'm just licking her juices from my fingers while she watches, still so fucking hard I think my cock could break a cinderblock in half.

"Answer me, Princess," I whisper.

"Yes," she says, her voice barely audible.

I turn her around and kiss her hard. I know I taste like her but I *want* her to taste herself on my lips, to know how much I like *devouring* her.

This might be the first time, but it won't be the

last.

"Good," I say. "Because I've got every intention of doing it again and again. Princess, I'm going to make you come in ways you've never even *thought* of."

I swallow hard, trying to keep the darkness inside in check.

Just because she let you get her off in the garden doesn't mean she'll like anything else, I remind myself.

Go slow. You have to go slow, because sweet Josephine doesn't deserve to experience it all at once.

But now she's looking at me again, her eyes wide and innocent but with that unnameable *hunger* deep inside, the spark that catches something inside me and burns my body from the inside out.

She didn't have to do any of this. She didn't have to let me kiss her, touch her, make her come while two people stood just *feet* away.

But she did. She did and she *liked* it, her juices flowing over my fingers and down her legs, her body trembling and jerking as she came hard, and now I crave her even *more*.

Princess Josephine runs one hand down my chest, her hand small and delicate and gentle, sliding between two buttons on my shirt, but I catch her wrist.

"Not now," I tell her, still keeping my voice low. "*Now* you go back to your bedchamber."

"But you didn't—"

"*Go*," I tell her, and step around her to open the bushes for her, holding back the sharp thorns and branches.

Reluctantly, the princess — *my* princess — steps through, back onto the moonlit path. She takes a deep breath, then finally seems to collect herself, looking around like she's been dreaming.

"It was lovely to run into you, Prince Leo," she finally says, and curtsies neatly.

"Likewise, a pleasure," I say, and bow.

Just before we walk in opposite directions, our eyes lock.

And I *swear* my sweet, innocent princess is smiling.

• • •

The second I'm through the door of my chambers, I've got my cock out and in my hand, and I lean back against the shut door as I stroke it.

Jesus, it's a relief. It's not what I want, but it's a fucking *relief* all the same.

I can't believe she was there, willing, ready and *so* wet for me and I didn't do anything about it. I could have bent Princess Josephine over and fucked her hard behind those bushes, while her father's men droned on about economics on the other side, and I didn't.

I've been with *dozens* of women. My reputation as the prince who's never left his castle? Not true. All it takes is the bare minimum of a disguise — a hat, some glasses — and I'd hit the city. Women *flock* to me, practically falling over each other to sit in my lap, touch my scar. I've gotten blowjobs in nearly every bar bathroom back in Szegravia.

But all I did was get Josephine off.

I stroke myself harder, my thick cock filling my hand. It's horrified more than one potential lay because of its size, but it's delighted way, *way* more.

I sigh explosively, the fire gathering in my lower belly. More than *anything* I need to sink my monster into my princess, feel her tight, hot channel around me. Listen to her *moan* with pleasure as I fill her slowly, the first man to ever be inside her

The *only* man to ever be inside her, one hand in her hair as I fuck her deep, finding that perfect spot that makes her *scream* my name as she submits to me completely, her tight little cunt spasming around my shaft as she comes—

I pump my fist one more time and then I come with a growl, cum arcing halfway across the room and landing on a throw rug as I gasp, my cock spurting again and again.

When it's over, I lean my head back against the door. I know the relief is only temporary, and I'll wake up hard as a rock tomorrow morning, dreaming of her soft, tight body under mine.

But for now, at least I can sleep.

• • •

The next morning, I'm informed by young man in palace livery that King Edward and Queen Carolina wish to have breakfast with me. I'm disappointed, because I was looking forward to seeing Josephine for breakfast, but it's not as if I can refuse her parents.

Particularly when they're the King and Queen.

I meet them in their private dining room, a sunlit space with its own kitchen that overlooks the garden.

As I walk in, I can't help but look for the spot where I was last night, and something tightens in my stomach, even as I think about Josephine, beautiful in the throes of ecstasy, her body so tight against my cock that it was nearly torture.

All while her father's advisors stood five feet away.

"Your Majesties," I say, glancing at the gardens one more time.

Both of them nod politely, and the King gestures at an empty chair, so I sit.

Be on your best fucking behavior, I tell myself. *Use the right fucking fork and the right fucking knife, you brute.*

A servant comes by and deposits a china teacup at

PARKER GREY

my elbow, and I pick it up, sipping as delicately as I can, even though it looks comical in my thick, scarred hands.

"Prince Leopold, I'll cut right to the chase," the King says. "You're here because you've expressed an interest in marrying my daughter Josephine."

"Yes," I say, forcing my voice to its politest tones.

"We believe that a match between our countries could be quite advantageous," he goes on. "Your father and mother, the King and Queen of Szegravia, have been close allies of ours for years. When the crown princess died, it shook us all deeply."

I swallow hard as something black and ugly begins to blossom inside me. I don't think about my older sister often. Not any more, at least. God knows I used to think about it almost constantly.

"Thank you," I say. "It was truly an ordeal."

They have no *fucking* clue. Nadia's death was only the beginning of it, because after the funeral was finished, after the mourning period was over, my parents were still broken people.

And me? I was the target for more than a decade's worth of speculation.

62

I was *ten* when it happened. A child. Not that it mattered to any of the wolves, jackals, and vultures that spread the rumors afterward.

"And we're sorry for what you've gone through since then," Queen Carolina says, her voice soft and gentle. For a moment, I'm amazed at how much Josephine sounds like her.

"Thank you," I say again. I know I've learned a thousand ways to say *thank you* in my life, but I can't think of any others right now.

"We would be pleased for you to marry Josephine, is what we're getting at," the King says.

The knot in my chest unravels a little.

"But we would never force our daughter to marry someone against her will," the Queen says. "And... I'm afraid that Josephine doesn't know your family like we do."

I swallow tea.

"Does she believe the rumors?" I ask.

She can't believe them that much, I think, flashing back to last night for the thousandth time.

"I think Josephine is uncertain," Queen Carolina says. "And to that end, we'd like for you to spend some time with her today."

I nearly laugh in her face.

That's it? That's *all*?

I thought they were going to tell me we'd been caught last night and send me home packing. I thought I'd be stuck stealing my princess away in the dead of night instead of marrying her in a full state ceremony.

But no. They want us to go on a *date*.

"I'd be delighted and honored," I say, taking another sip of my tea like a goddamn fancy gentleman.

Chapter Nine

Josephine

Prince Leo picks up a finger sandwich. His back is perfectly rigid, and he looks at it like it's suspicious, some sort of strange, exotic food.

Then he takes a single, dainty, careful bite. It looks completely ridiculous, because he's *huge* and the sandwich is so tiny, but it's oddly sweet.

I know he's only here, trying to be polite and civilized, because of me, and because we've got two lunch attendants right now, watching us.

"These are very good," he growls.

"I'll give your compliments to the chef," I say.

When I told my parents that I needed to spend more time with Prince Leo, this wasn't *exactly* what I meant, being watched by the staff while we eat finger sandwiches. But it's better than nothing, and no matter what my body is telling me right now, we need to have conversations *once* in a while.

Though admittedly, just staring at his hands and knowing what they can *do* has me wet.

And I can't stop fantasizing about him pushing me down on this table. *Commanding* me to bend over for him, his thick *monstrous* cock nudging against my slick, wet opening.

I want him to *distraction*, and I've never wanted anyone before.

"This game preserve is quite nice," he says, conversationally. "What sort of game do you hunt here?"

"Oh, *I* don't hunt," I say, laughing a little. "In fact, hardly anyone does any more. There are some deer and maybe a flock of pheasants, but it's been a long time since anyone actually shot one."

He lifts one eyebrow, leaning forward slightly.

"Why?" he asks.

I shrug.

"It seems a little uncivilized," I say. "Unsporting, maybe? To keep nearly-tame animals on your land and then shoot them for fun."

"I see," he says.

"Does Szegravia still have the game preserve?" I ask.

"It's also in disuse," he says. "Though we've not kept up the paths or the buildings like you have. I'm afraid it's gone back to nature, nothing but wilderness. Every few years we have to hack it back before it overruns the castle."

I frown slightly, looking down at the table, then turn my head to the waiter, standing attentively at the end of the table.

"I think we're ready for dessert now, please," I say.

He nods professionally, then walks away. We're in a building that was once a greenhouse, used to grow flowers and vegetables, though now it's simply a pleasant place to spend an afternoon.

"I'd rather have *you* for dessert, Princess," Leo growls once the man is gone.

I blush bright red. Even though I *knew* what would happen, and even though all day he's been whispering filthy things to me whenever we're out of the attendants' earshot, I can't help but have this reaction.

"You're meant to be proving yourself to me as a royal gentleman," I murmur.

He smiles, and it's almost *feral*.

"I've been the *perfect* gentleman where it counts," he says, a half-smile creeping over his face. "Princess, all *day* I've been behaving myself impeccably, if I may say so."

I look down at the table. It's true. When Prince Leo *wants* to be, he's literally everything I could wish for in a prince: handsome, charming, perfectly mannered. He even threw his jacket over a mud puddle that was in my path this morning.

But I've still got this lingering, nagging sense of doubt. Leo in person is *so* different from the Leo of rumor and conjecture that I've heard about, again and again.

There's no *possible* way he could be the monster he's alleged to be, right? He's a little uncouth, not a killer.

I play with a fork on the table, rotating it between my fingers hesitantly. I know that I just need to ask, but I don't know how to form the words.

"You're still afraid of me," he says simply, and I look up at him, into his scarred face, his deep, beautiful eyes.

"No," I say, and I'm not lying. "I was. I'm not now, but…"

I take a deep breath.

"I've heard things and I need to know the truth," I tell him.

We're both silent for a moment, and the servant standing at the end of the table shifts uncomfortably. I dismiss him with a nod of my head, and he disappears through a door into the kitchen.

Leo leans back in his chair, his rigid posture and manners shifting, the perfect courtly prince disappearing and something *real* taking his place.

"The truth is that Nadia's death was my fault," he says quietly.

I can't breathe, like a giant fist is closed around my lungs.

"Even though she was two years older than me, I was always the instigator," he goes on. "Nadia was quiet, well-behaved, always had her nose in a book, but I was a wild little hellion."

He taps the tongs on the fork on the table.

"We were inseparable anyway, and we'd taken to exploring the castle when no one was watching us — and since I was ten and she was twelve, she was judged capable of keeping me out of trouble. And instead, one afternoon, I talked her into exploring the ruined tower."

He pauses briefly, staring at the fork.

"We weren't supposed to be there. It was structurally unsound from a fire a hundred years before, but I talked her into it. And when she walked to look at the view from the edge, it crumbled underneath her."

His eyes are bright at the memory, and a pang stabs through my heart. He's never looked more *human*.

"And I *caught* her," he says quietly. "But I couldn't hold on, and I had to watch as she fell to her death."

"I'm sorry," I whisper, knowing that it's not enough.

"I got the scar then, too," he says. "I didn't realize until hours later that I'd nearly lost my eye to an old nail sticking out of a wall where I threw myself down."

He shifts again in his seat, puts the fork down, and looks me square in the eye.

"My parents told the press that I hadn't been there, that Nadia had been on her own, because they didn't want it to look suspicious. But of course someone had seen the two of us together, and it eventually got out that I was there, and it only looked *more* suspicious, like at ten years old I'd killed my own sister so I could inherit the kingdom."

He shrugs lightly.

"They were too deep in their grief to care much about public relations, and I just wanted to crawl into a hole and never come out, so the rumor mill got to run full force with no one to stop it," he finishes.

I know the rest, of course.

"I didn't believe it," I say, swallowing hard. "But I didn't *not* believe it."

Leo smiles and stands, then comes around the table and pulls me to my feet.

"Do you believe me now?" he asks.

A shiver slides down my spine.

"I do," I whisper.

"Good," he murmurs. "I couldn't stand it if you thought I was a monster."

The intimacy of this moment combined with his sheer proximity is making heat wind through my body yet again, finally unfettered by the thought that Leo might be *dangerous*.

The attendant comes back and sets tray of dainty desserts on the table, and I clear my throat.

"After luncheon, I think Prince Leo and I would prefer to take a stroll through the preserve alone," I tell the attendant.

He frowns.

"Princess, your father did say—"

"Prince Leo and I have some very important matters to discuss," I say firmly. "My father will understand."

He nods.

Prince Leo's eyes sparkle dangerously.

. . .

A few minutes later, we're walking away from the greenhouse and along a path into the well-kept woods of the game preserve. It's a vast expanse of land behind the castle, up in the hills where it's impossible to farm anything anyway.

We make small talk at first, my stomach in knots. I've thrown caution to the wind, because even though I *still* don't know whether the rumors about the prince are true, and I *still* think he might be the sort of wild, feral, untamed beast that everyone thinks he is, I'm here alone with him.

The moment we're out of sight of the greenhouse, he grabs me in his arms and lifts me. I yelp, but the noise is swallowed by the trees and the ground, so I wrap my arms around his neck and hold my breath.

"You afraid of something, Princess?" he asks, his voice a low growl.

I swallow.

Yes, I think. *I'm a little afraid of you and a lot afraid of what I'll do when you're around.*

"No," I squeak.

He puts me down on a fallen tree so I'm straddling it in my short sundress, and he towers over me. Out of habit, I try to pull my dress down, but Leo just laughs and pushes my hands away.

"That's not what you're here for," he says, kissing me hard. "You didn't send your men away so you could stay *modest*, did you, Princess?"

I can't even answer because his mouth is on mine again, practically crushing me, the force of his desire almost overwhelming. His tongue invades my mouth without permission, plundering me and exploring every part.

It's aggressive. It's *dominating*. I like it, and I like having him inside me.

And I want *more*.

Leo is pushing me backward, my arms holding me up against the fallen tree, and his mouth leaves mine and moves lower. Down my neck, past my collarbone.

Roughly he shoves the neckline of my dress down and I gasp, my bra suddenly exposed, but Leo just chuckles and pushes that down, too, his lips finding the puckered pink of one nipple.

He bites it gingerly, and I *gasp*, the sensation zipping through my body like I've been electrocuted. I can't believe how *good* this feels, and his other hand comes up, shoves my bra away, and pinches the other nipple at the same time.

"Leo," I whisper.

He bites a little harder, and my toes *curl*.

Then he reaches down and under my skirt, his rough hand moving up my thigh, his fingers sliding underneath my panties.

"You're soaking goddamn wet, Princess," he says, his voice low and rough. "Is that for me?"

"Yes," I whisper.

His fingers slide across my lips, slippery with my juices.

"Is this because I said I was going to tongue-fuck you while you moaned?" he asks. "Or is this because you've been staring at my thick royal cock all day?"

I clear my throat, breathing hard.

"The first one?"

He just chuckles and takes my hand, guiding it to the impossibly big, hard rod in his pants. I *gasp*.

"That's a pity," he says. "Because they're *both* good reasons for your panties to be soaked straight through."

He grabs my panties in one hand and *yanks*, tearing them off and tossing them to the forest floor before I can even speak. Then Prince Leo kisses me even harder, pushing me backward until I'm lying on the fallen tree, legs around him as he presses his rock-hard *need* against me.

His lips travel down again, past my neck, my breasts, my belly, and then he's shoving my dress over my hips, his hands tight on my thighs.

Something runs the length of my lips, something deft and flexible.

It *has* to be his tongue.

He does it again, teasing me, only this time he pushes his tongue between them and laps at my entrance, coming *so* close to entering me but he doesn't. Instead he flattens it and slides it to my clit, where he licks me in slow, deft circles.

My toes curl, and I *gasp*. Holy *fuck* this feels good, and even if I can't believe I'm letting him do this right here, right *now*, I couldn't stop for the world.

It's total, pure ecstasy, and I reach both my hands over my head and grab onto a branch stump behind myself as he licks at me, his tongue gliding over my most intimate places while I gasp and squirm, his strong hands holding my thighs open wide.

We're right out, in the open, where *anyone* could come along and see. And yet I'm completely powerless to stop, totally under his control in his moment, my body writhing like a river of fire is flowing through me.

Leo's tongue is fast and merciless, and I've *never* had anyone do this to me before. In no time at all, I'm teetering on the brink of orgasm, moments away from falling over that sweet edge and coming hard, but then his tongue slows.

I hold my breath, but he doesn't start again, just draws slow circles *around* my clit until the sensation fades and I'm not at that dangerous edge any more.

Then he starts again, pushing me right up to the edge, and backing off.

He's teasing me. No, worse: he's *torturing* me, making sure I know he has the power to make me come whenever he wants, but he's not giving me the satisfaction. I feel like sparks in a windstorm, hot and swirling, my body a rush of confusion and pleasure and pure, desperate *want*.

The next time he does it, I'm so close that I think I might come anyway, just from the sheer force of my desire. I stay at the brink even after his tongue leaves me, this time sliding down, between my lips as I whimper *desperately*, my whole body trembling.

Then, at *last*, he slides his tongue inside me and curls it *hard* against my sensitive front wall, and I *explode*. My back arches and my toes curl as pleasure arcs through me like lightning, fast and hard, but it keeps moving and going long past the point where I've been struck.

The sensation sizzles through my veins over and over again, until at last my legs are shaking, my breath coming in quick gasps, and I'm almost delirious.

Leo moves his face away from me, kissing and biting my inner thigh, then my belly, then my lips as I'm still laid back on the fallen tree. I kiss back like a drowning woman, even though he tastes like me, because I don't *care*.

After a long time I sit up, dazed, Leo's lips still on mine. From pure instinct I try to slide my hand down his body, because I *want* him, want to see his thick, monstrous cock and make him feel as good as he's made me, but he catches my wrist.

Then he moves his face away from mine and grins, just as I hear footsteps on dry leaves coming through the forest.

"Not now, Princess," he murmurs.

Frantically, I pull up the top of my dress and pull down the bottom, sitting upright on the fallen tree as Leo sits next to me, just as casual as can be.

I can only pray that we're hiding my torn panties from whoever's on the path, and hold my breath. Leo takes one of my hands in his own, like he's a dutiful, polite suitor, not the *beast* who just ate me out right here in the woods.

An older man comes into view. I think I recognize him from the stables — he isn't someone I see every day, but he's familiar.

He nods at us. We nod at him, and he continues his walk.

Then Leo pulls me up and leads me back to the greenhouse where we had lunch. Despite everything, I'm disappointed — I want to feel what it's like when *he* comes so hard he can't control himself, when *he* writhes and jerks with pleasure.

But I understand that now's not the time.

Chapter Ten

Leo

Lying awake in my bed, I swear I can still taste her on my lips.

I've eaten a meal since then, drunk water, drunk wine, had dessert, and brushed my teeth. There's no *way* I can still taste her sweet honey in my mouth, but I'd swear I can.

And it's driving me *absolutely* crazy. I haven't thought of anything else at all since this afternoon. Not her parents, talking to me; not the other nobles currently at the palace; not where I was walking or what I was eating or drinking.

Just my tongue, licking at her while she gasped and writhed. The way it felt to push my tongue inside her, to feel her muscles clamp down on me when she came like that.

Fucking *glorious*. I've never felt anything like it before, not even close — the way my sweet princess was totally, completely, and utterly *mine* in that moment.

I roll over, still not asleep, and sigh.

I wonder if she's still awake, I think.

In her bed. Naked. Maybe thinking about me.

It's past midnight, in a palace that mostly goes to sleep early except for the guards, who are *everywhere*. I'm likely to wake her up, freak her out, and she'll probably call them.

And fuck it, I don't *care*.

I need her *now*, and I need her worse than ever. I can't sleep, think, or hardly even *breathe* until I'm with her again, so I get out of my bed, put on a fresh set of clothes, and step quietly into the hall, closing my door behind me.

No one here. So far, so good.

I've not been to her chambers yet but I know where they are, so I head that way. I pass a few guards in the portrait gallery, but I just nod at them, like I can't sleep and I'm out for a midnight stroll. They just nod back.

Finally, I'm at her door. At least, I'm fairly sure it's her door, though it's not as if her name is on it. I can't believe there aren't more guards here, but I guess the palace is fairly safe. Besides, most threats come from *outside* the palace walls.

I raise my hand to knock, then let it fall. If I make noise, I just risk alerting everyone that I'm here, paying Josephine a visit at twelve-thirty at night with a raging hard-on.

It's risky — she might scream — but I lower my hand to the handle, and I push.

It's unlocked. That sort of makes sense — she's got guards, after all, though they certainly didn't stop me.

I step through her door silently, blood rushing through my veins in sheer anticipation. Every nerve in my body feels alive, tingling with danger but mostly with pure *excitement*.

I walk through the first room in her chambers, some kind of living room or sitting room or something, totally silent, heading for her bedroom.

The door is slightly ajar, so I say a quick prayer and push it open.

As I do, there's a rustle and a *gasp,* then total stillness.

"It's me," I say, keeping my voice low. "I needed to see you again. *Tonight.*"

For a moment, I just pray that I got the right room. I'll happily withstand any physical attack to be with Josephine, but showing up in her little sister's bedroom would *really* take some apologizing and explaining.

But then Josephine sits up in her bed, hair wild around her face. She's holding her bedsheets up in front of her, but underneath the thin silk I can tell that she's completely naked.

For a moment, she just takes me in, still sleepy and confused, and she runs her tongue just under her top lip.

"Leo," she finally whispers, drawing her feet up under her.

I walk forward like I'm magnetized. Through the thin sheets I can watch her nipples harden quickly, an expression of deep *lust* coming into her beautiful blue eyes as her breathing quickens.

"You can't be here," she murmurs, looking up at me.

"Apparently, I can," I say, stepping up to the edge of her bed. I feel like my body is on *fire*, nothing but thin fabric separating me from my princess.

"You shouldn't," she whispers. "We're not married yet, and you know my parents..."

I run my fingers along her chin, and she tilts her head up, melting into my touch.

"*Yet*?" I say, voice low and gravelly with need.

Her eyes hold mine steadily, and I run the pad of my thumb over her full, plush lips as I guide my head to the back of her head.

"There's no wedding date yet," she whispers against my thumb. "But I'm yours, Leo."

I feel like something inside me goes supernova at those three simple words: *I'm yours, Leo*. I can't even respond, the feeling is so powerful, but Josephine opens her lips slightly and runs the tip of her tongue along the pad of my finger.

It sends tingles down my spine, my breathing growing heavy. After a moment she opens her mouth wider, sucking my thumb into her mouth up to the first joint, her tongue swirling around it, then the second, then down to where it meets my hand. The whole time she doesn't break eye contact with me, the soft satin of the bed sheets against her lithe, gorgeous body.

I'm uncontrollably hard, and in that moment, the last thing thread that held the beast inside me in check *snaps*. I pull my thumb from her beautiful mouth and lock my hand in her hair, *just* hard enough that she knows who's in control but she's not hurt.

Josephine lets the sheets slide down her body, exposing her full, perky breasts with their rosy nipples, her waist, her hips. The soft, downy patch between her thighs.

"Get on your knees," I growl, already unbuckling my belt with my other hand.

Josephine locks eyes with me, and something flickers in her gaze, some light that comes on when I grab her hair and tell her what to do.

Then she *smiles*, just barely, a coy little smirk that stokes my raging fire even more.

"Yes, my Prince," she whispers, and slides off her bed.

Then her hands are on the waist of my pants, her lips on the trail of fur that leads from my bellybutton to my cock, and she pulls my trousers open hungrily, like she's been *waiting* for this.

Josephine unzips my pants, and my cock *springs* out, enormous and bulging, the head swollen and purple with desire.

She *gasps*.

"You've never seen one before," I say.

"Not in person," she whispers.

I can tell she's nervous, but she wraps one hand around the base of it, her fingers barely closing around my shaft, and it sends a bolt of white-hot electricity through my entire body as she strokes me slowly and carefully.

"You like it?" I growl.

Josephine just nods, my hand still locked in her hair.

"Good," I say, and tilt her head back slightly, her creamy throat exposed. "Because it's yours, Princess. From now on, every single inch of me belongs to *you*."

Her hand tightens on my shaft, and she strokes me a little faster.

"Now open your pretty mouth, because I *need* to see your lips wrapped around my cock," I say.

Chapter Eleven

Josephine

Oh my *God*, it's big. I know I've never touched a cock before, but I've gotten curious enough to find pictures of them. I'm familiar with the concept of cocks, if not the practice.

But I was *not* prepared, because Prince Leo is *huge*. As much as I've been fantasizing about this moment, and even though I had to get myself off three times before I could fall asleep, suddenly I'm uncertain.

I'm not sure I can fit this in my mouth, and I'm a *virgin...*

...there's no way he's going to fit.

"I *need* to see your lips wrapped around my cock," he growls, his voice so rough and gritty that it sends chills down my spine.

Leo tilts my head back, just a few degrees, but something about the motion makes heat flood down through my body, my pussy getting even wetter with that simple gesture.

He's in control right now, totally dominant. I'm *his*.

And I *like* it.

Tentatively, I open my mouth, stick out my tongue, and carefully lick along the underside of his cock. Leo *groans*, his fist tightening in my hair, so I do it again.

Then I open as wide as I can and suck his cock into my mouth.

"*Fuck* that feels good, Princess," he growls as I pull my head back, swirling my tongue around the thick, bulbous head of his cock. I plunge my mouth back down, my lips sliding down the shaft, and I take Leo in as far as I possibly can.

It's nowhere *near* the whole thing, but he groans all the same, and I keep going, bobbing my head up and down on him, trying to take him deeper with every stroke, but he's hitting the back of my mouth.

And I *like* it. My God, do I like this: on my knees,

naked while he's almost fully clothed, submitting to Leo's control. I'm so wet that I can feel it dripping down my thighs in a near-flood, just from pleasuring this man.

"You're so *fucking* beautiful right now, Princess," he says, breathlessly. "I swear, watching you suck my cock is the most beautiful thing I've seen in my whole life."

I just suck harder, his cock pulsing and throbbing in my mouth and in the hand I've still got wrapped around his shaft, stroking him.

"I'm gonna come," he says. "And you're going to swallow every last drop and then lick me clean, Princess."

A wave of butterflies parades through my stomach, and I look up at him, but he's got his head thrown back, every muscle tensed and knotted.

Then his hand tightens in my hair until it *hurts*, and even though tears spring to my eyes I *like* it, shocks of pleasure rippling down my spine as he pushes my mouth onto his cock as far as I can take it.

And he *explodes*, jolting and throbbing in my mouth, and all I can do is swallow again and again as he shoots stream after stream down my throat.

Gradually, it ends. His hand on my head relaxes, and I pull my mouth back slowly, licking and sucking as I go because I *want* to clean every last drop from him. I *love* having him inside me, and in that moment I want to give him *everything* that I can.

I want Prince Leo to have my body, *all* of it. I want to pleasure him in every single way possible.

"Stand up," he growls, once I've licked him clean.

I obey, and for a long moment, he just looks me over. His cock is still hard, still standing at attention, and yet another thrill rides through me.

I want it. I want *him*, that enormous beast, inside me. Stretching me out and stuffing me full until I *scream* with pleasure.

"Get on the bed," he commands, his voice soft but steely.

I sit, and he gestures me back, so I move onto the bed and lay down, watching him.

He stuff his cock back into his pants, and doesn't take them off. In fact, he does his belt again, and a jolt of disappointment moves through my body.

"Spread your legs for me and let me see your

pretty little cunt," he murmurs.

I blush at the word, a word I *never* thought would make me wet, but it does. I take a deep breath and spread my legs for him as he kneels between my thighs, his hands roaming over my body, squeezing my breasts, rolling my nipples between his thick fingers.

I moan quietly. I can't help it. I'm soaking wet and trembling with desire, totally helpless against the potent combination of my own desperate desire and this *dominating* man.

Prince Leo growls, the low noise coming from somewhere deep in his chest, and runs his thumb over my dripping, drooling slit.

"Did sucking my cock make you this wet, Princess?" he asks.

"Yes," I whisper.

"You're so fucking sexy when you swallow my cum," he goes on, voice raspy and rough. "And you're so fucking sexy when you come with your thighs around my head."

He laps at me, once, and I shiver.

"And I can't fucking *wait* for you to come with

my thick cock buried inside your tight little pussy," he whispers, one finger nudging between my lips, stroking my entrance. "Because your mouth is mine, Princess. And your pussy will be mine."

His slick fingers drift away from my lips, *down*, until they're on my puckered back hole, and I hold my breath. I can't *believe* he's touching me there. It's so *dirty*.

But I like it.

"And your ass will be mine, too," he says. "Not yet, but soon."

I draw in a deep, shuddering breath as he moves his fingers back to my entrance.

"Please," I say. "I need you, *now*, please."

He just laughs.

"Not yet," he says. "Not until we're married. *Then* I'll take your sweet, virgin pussy, but not yet."

I open my mouth to beg again, but before I can say anything his mouth is between my legs and he's licking me, fiercely, his tongue rough and gentle and fucking *perfect* all at once. All I can do is moan as he sends me spiraling higher and higher, toward that perfect cliff.

I'm afraid he's just going to tease me again, get me close again and again like he did before but he doesn't. This time, just as I'm about to come, he puts his lips around my clit and sucks *hard*, still teasing me with his tongue.

I *shout*, my toes curling and my hands clutching my sheets for dear life as I shatter into a million pieces, each one shaking with the sheer force of my orgasm. I can't move and I can barely *think*, it feels so good, but Leo doesn't stop.

His tongue circles my clit slowly, then laps across it, each stroke getting another jolt out of me, and before I know it's he's shifted on the bed, tongue still flicking back and forth, as something *else* strokes my slit.

Then he slides between my lips as I hold my breath, and in moments, his finger is *inside* me, teasing, stroking at my wall and I moan again.

"That feels so good," I whisper, still panting for breath.

Leo doesn't answer, just keep licking me and adds another finger. This time I bite my lip, because it feels so *good* to have him fill me like this, stretching my virgin channel a little further than it's ever been stretched before.

I've used my own fingers, of course, but it didn't feel *anything* like this, rough and dominating and oh so *good*.

"More," I pant. "Please, Leo."

He pulls back, his tongue still moving, and he strokes my entrance. I'm practically gushing juices, his face shining with them, and then, slowly, he slides three fingers into me.

I can't move. This is more than I've ever had before, and I've got the sensation that I'm as full as I can get, totally stuffed, and it feels *incredible*. He moves his fingers and strokes me, and before I know what I'm doing I'm writhing and rolling my hips, trying to fuck his hand as hard as I can.

I come again in *seconds*, and this time I've got my hands locked in his hair, moaning his name, and he *still* doesn't stop, not until I've come one more time.

Now I feel drained, limp, like there's no possible way I can *move*, let alone come again.

Leo finally stops licking me, though he doesn't pull his fingers out.

"Satisfied, Princess?" he asks.

I just swallow hard and nod, even though it's not quite true. I *still* want his cock inside me, even though I know it won't be happening tonight.

But he just chuckles.

"Roll over," he says.

I don't move, because I don't understand, and I just look down at his face, the forbidding scar standing out even in the moonlight.

"Princess," he growls. "Roll *over*."

I lift myself on my elbows, and I turn over carefully. His fingers never leave my pussy, and with every degree I turn I can feel them inside me, finding my sensitive spots and sending sparks of pleasure through my body.

The second I'm on my belly, he grabs my hips with his other hand and pulls me back so I'm kneeling again, knees wide, totally and completely open and vulnerable to him.

Leo starts fucking me with his fingers again, slow and deep, hitting *exactly* the right spot inside me to make me moan, my face buried in a pillow. In moments I'm moving too, pushing myself back against his hand as I pretend that it's his cock buried deep inside me.

With his other hand, he grabs my ass.

And *then* I feel his tongue, warm and wet, probing my back hole.

I *gasp* and freeze, because I suddenly have no idea what to do. He said he'd claim my ass, but I didn't think he meant with his *tongue*.

This is dirty, absolutely *filthy* beyond anything I'd ever imagined. I've never even touched myself there, and even though I know people like it, it just seems... *wrong*.

But then his tongue moves in a slow circle, and it feels *so* good.

I know I shouldn't like it, but I *do*, no matter how disgusting and dirty it is. Leo's fingers keep moving and I moan, leaning back, his fingers inside me and his tongue on my ass, completely and totally filthy.

I come so hard I don't even make noise, just hold my breath as every muscle in my body tenses. Leo just groans in response, his fingers and tongue moving faster and harder, and in that moment I don't *care* that I'm being dominated and fucked, I just *love* it.

And I love *him*.

When I finish, he finally pulls away, and I slump to the bed, face first. I can hear him slurping my juices from his fingers, his other hand wandering up my spine to the back of my neck.

But still, I'm surprised when he kisses me. It's gentle and *tender*, sweet and soft after he grabbed my hair like that and then finger-fucked me four ways from Sunday.

"Thank you," I whisper.

"I"m yours, Princess," he whispers back, lying next to me and rolling us onto our sides so we can spoon. "And I'll always be yours. From now until forever."

"And I'm yours," I whisper back. "I promise."

For some reason, that simple exchange feels better than ten thousand orgasms.

Chapter Twelve

Leo

It's not exactly a surprise when, a week later, Josephine's parents invite me to tea and inform me that they've decided to accept my offer of marriage to their middle daughter.

I knew she'd say yes. She's been saying *yes* every night, over and over again, when I sneak to her chambers after dark.

The days between our nights together are *torture*. I thought that maybe her sweet mouth on my swollen cock would alleviate some of the raging desire inside me, but it's only intensified. I only have to watch Josephine walk into a room and I'm hard as rock.

My pants are all about ready to burst at the seams. I've considered taping my dick down more than once, because it's only a matter of time before this situation gets incredibly awkward.

The wedding is set for a month from now, and even though I could easily go back home between now and then, I make up some excuse to stay in Tomassia until then — I'm the acting Szegravian envoy or some shit, I don't know.

I just know that every time I see Josephine, it gets harder and harder to keep her virginity intact. I promised her, and I can't explain exactly why I want to wait until we're married to finally fuck her, but I *do*.

Call me a romantic, but I like the thought that I'll only enter her as her husband.

Her *king*.

But every time I visit her at night, when I make her come with my hands and my tongue, when she straddles me while she strokes my cock, breasts bouncing as she does, it gets harder to keep that promise.

And resisting while Josephine is wet and willing in front of me, her perfect, beautiful body prone, and she *begs* me to take her?

It's the hardest fucking thing I've ever done.

• • •

A week after we're officially engaged, I sneak back to her chambers. By now I'm barely sneaking, and I'm nearly sure that some of the guards know what we're up to, but I'm not sure they care.

After all, we're set to be married. Her father would still be absolutely *furious*, but he doesn't need to know.

I open Josephine's door, close it quickly behind myself, and look around.

She's not in her sitting room. Usually she is, naked and ready for me. Last night she was right there in that chair, and without speaking I took my belt off, tied her hands behind her, and she sucked my cock before I bent her over the chair, still bound, and drank her honey until she could barely move.

I've learned that my princess *likes* being dominated. She loves it when I tie her up like that, when I get a little rough, and the way she submits practically brings me to my knees with lust.

I walk through that room and into the next,

pushing her bedroom door open quietly. She's standing in front of her full-length mirror, and when she hears me, she turns.

I stop breathing.

I don't know *where* she got it, but she's wearing a tight, white, translucent sleeveless dress over a tiny white thong and white thigh-high fishnet stockings. Every curve of her body is visible, her perfect rosy nipples poking through the thin fabric.

I swear to God I can hear the fabric of my trousers straining, because there's just something *about* lingerie. She's fucking beautiful naked, but the sheer knowledge that she dressed like this *just* to make my dick this hard, well...

...It's working.

"Do you like it?" Josephine asks, smiling shyly. I know she's never dressed up like this for anyone before, so I'm sure she's nervous, but I don't *care*.

I just *grunt*, crossing her bedroom in one second flat, grabbing her and *crushing* my mouth against hers. A low, feral noise comes from somewhere deep in my chest as her arms wind around me, her skin warm through her flimsy dress.

I push her against the wall, already rolling her nipples between my fingers while she moans into my mouth, writhing against me, and I hitch one of her legs around my waist, pulling her tiny thong aside.

Soaking goddamn wet, not that I'm surprised. Josephine exhales in a sigh and moves her hips against my hand, like she's trying to push my fingers inside her, and she looks up at me as she bites her lip.

I lose control.

I back away, grab her, spin her around. She's got a mirror vanity next to her closet and I bend her roughly over that, both our faces visible as I rip her thong off.

"Leo," she moans, and her eyes meet mine in the mirror, two pools of pure *lust*. "Please."

Before I know what I'm doing, my cock is out and in my hand, and I push Josephine forward a little further, parting her thighs roughly so she's got one knee on the vanity, practically laying on it.

God, I can *smell* how turned on she is by this, her perfect pussy pink and dripping, open and exposed.

Mine.

I grip my cock by the base and slide it along her

lips as she moans again, my other hand on her back, but I don't enter her. I want to, dear *God* do I want to, but I don't.

"Please," she whimpers again.

I swallow hard, nudging the tip of my cock against her clit, feeling her body thrum in response.

"Please what?" I growl.

"Please fuck me," she begs. Even though she still blushes if I say *cunt*, sweet Josephine has developed her vocabulary lately. "Leo, I *need* you inside me."

I don't respond, but I keep teasing her clit with the head of my cock, back and forth. Her eyes flutter closed and she bites her lip again, then whimpers.

"Leo."

Now I'm at her entrance again. All it would take is *one* thrust, *one* subtle motion of my hips and I'd finally be inside my perfect, tempting princess.

But I don't. Even though I want it more than almost anything in the world, I don't. Instead I bend down, put my mouth on her clit, and lick her until she comes hard, moaning.

When she finishes, I pull her to standing and kiss her, but she won't meet my eyes until I take her by the chin and force her to look up.

"I said you'd be a virgin until your wedding night, and I meant it," I say.

She swallows and looks down, dejected.

"We're *engaged*," she says.

"I want to take your virginity as your *husband*," I say, and I've never meant anything more. "I want to be your first and your last, and I want you to *know* that I mean it."

"I know," she whispers.

I pause for a moment, turning over the idea that I had a few minutes ago.

It might be reckless, it might be dumb, and it might piss some people off.

But I think I'm past caring.

"Let's elope," I say.

Chapter Thirteen

Josephine

SEVEN MILES TO MONTBLANCHE, the
sign reads.

I bite my lip again and watch the headlights pool
in the road out of Leo's windshield, dark towns and
houses whizzing by.

I can't *believe* I'm doing this. I can't *believe* I'm
getting married now, at nearly one o'clock in the
morning, without my parents' approval. I've never
really done *anything* without their approval — least
of all marry someone.

I look over at Leo, and he looks back at me, the
scar on his face shining in the reflection of his
headlights, and he grins.

Then he takes my hand in his and kisses it, and I
grin back.

I'm still not sure how this happened, how I fell in love with a man who terrified me a couple of weeks ago, but I did. Somewhere between toe-curling orgasms, we stayed in my bed and *talked* until three or four in the morning.

I told him about my strict family, about growing up in one of the smallest but wealthiest nations in the world. About the constant fear that one of our bigger, more powerful neighbors might decide to invade one day, and we'd likely be out of luck.

He talks about the years after his sister died, when his parents both turned inward and practically left him to fend for himself, when he stopped leaving his castle for a while and that's when all the rumors blossomed. He talks about feeling like a monster, about starting to believe everything that was said about him. Thinking that maybe he really *was* that man.

Montblanche is a city on the border of Tomassia and Luchenne, a sort of European Las Vegas where everything is open twenty-four hours and you don't need to apply for a marriage license more than five minutes in advance.

Leo pulls into the first wedding chapel he sees, one barely across the international border. My heart is *hammering* in my chest, my mind racing as he shuts off the engine and cuts the headlights.

Should I do this? Is this stupid?

Am I getting married at one in the morning in Montblanche just so we can have sex?

Then I look over, into Leo's eyes, and all my fears dissolve.

This *is* crazy. It *might* be stupid, and it's definitely reckless.

But I know, deep down, that it's not the *wrong* thing.

"You ready?" he asks, kissing my hand again.

I smile, even as a whole troupe of bats flutters through my stomach, I'm so nervous.

"Ready," I say.

• • •

If the people running the wedding chapel in Montblanche recognize us, they do a good job of not saying anything. It makes me wonder *how* many famous people, or how many royals at least, get married at times and place like this.

Maybe more than I thought.

Getting married is surprisingly easy. We fill out some forms, pick rings, I pick flowers, and then suddenly it's *happening*.

The whole ceremony is a blur, and I feel a little like I'm floating above myself, watching someone else get married. As excited as I am, it doesn't seem *real*.

At least, not until the very end.

"I do," Leo says, staring deep into my eyes, my hands locked in his.

I swallow hard. The officiant asks me if I promise to love and cherish, honor and obey, et cetera. My heart's beating too loudly for me to really hear him.

"I do," I say, my voice barely more than a whisper.

"You may now kiss the bride," he intones.

Leo slides one hand along my jaw, cupping my face tenderly, and lowers his lips to mine. It's the gentlest kiss we've ever exchanged, almost tentative, sweet and loving and tender.

It still makes my knees weak. Leo runs his tongue along my lip and I open my mouth under his, wrapping my arms around him as his other hand makes its way to my lower back, bringing me in against his body.

He's *rock* hard. I bite his lip gently as he pulls away, smiling down at me dotingly, like any good husband.

Even though the officiant is standing *right* there, he's not really paying any attention to us. Leo ends the kiss, then leans in, his lips against my ear.

"I'm going to fill you up with my thick cock and make you come until sunrise," he whispers.

I blush *bright* red, because even if I've gotten a little more use to his dirty talk, he usually doesn't do it *in front of people*. But no one else seems to notice, and Leo smiles at me, then at them, and we walk back down the aisle.

• • •

Ten minutes later, we're walking down the hall of the hotel attached to the chapel, part of our wedding package. I'm giddy and breathless, because I can't *believe* I'm married, and I'm also quivering in anticipation for what's about to happen.

Leo takes out the key, puts it in the lock, and turns it.

Then he turns to *me*, the two of us alone in this hotel hallway.

"Josephine, I love you," he says, and his voice is tender and gentle. "And as much as you're *mine*, I'm *yours*, from the day I met you until the day I die."

He kisses me.

"I couldn't be happier that someday you'll be my queen and the mother of our children," he goes on. "And I wanted you to know that, right here, right now, as crazy as this may seem, when I say forever I *mean* it."

"I mean it too," I whisper.

We kiss one more time, our tongues tangling together, the familiar heat building up inside me. The kiss starts out gentle but gets rougher as it goes, until Leo's hands are on my ass, squeezing and lifting through the dress I hurriedly put on a few hours ago.

We're still in the middle of the hallway as he

slides his fingers between my buttocks, quickly moving over my back hole and plunging between my lips, reveling in my wetness.

I swallow hard.

"*Now* will you finally fuck me?" I whisper.

Leo grins and pushes open the door.

Chapter Fourteen

Leo

I kick the door closed behind us, and it slams loudly but I don't fucking care. Already I'm tearing at Josephine's clothes, pulling her dress off over her head, pushing her into the hotel room as I throw her bra into a corner.

It's not a particularly fancy hotel, but it's not terrible. I couldn't care less how many stars it has, though; as long as Josephine's here, I'll be *anywhere*.

"Leo," she gasps again as I lift her up and place her on the bed. She's already naked, her hands scrabbling at my shirt before I pull it off over my head.

I kiss her roughly, her mouth soft and pliant and *needy* under mine as her hands grope for my belt, but I grab her by the wrists and pull her hands behind her, *towering* over her small, soft body.

She makes me feel like an animal, something feral and *wild*, but in a good way, and as I pull back, I can see her eyes light up as she wraps her legs around me, pulling me in.

I keep a hold on her wrists with one hand, and with the other, I undo my belt and then pull it out of my belt loops. Josephine doesn't say anything, just watches me, chest heaving as I pull her hands in front of her again.

"Tonight we do things *my* way, Princess," I growl, wrapping my belt around her wrists. "And my way is I fuck you when I like, *how* I like, because I've been *craving* your sweet body from the second I first saw you."

Josephine bites her lip as I fasten my belt around her wrists, tight enough that she can't get them apart, and then she looks up at me, her eyes filled with lust and longing. She knows *exactly* what I've got in store for her, and she wants it *just* as bad as I do.

I shove her bound hands over her head again and kiss her fiercely, my tongue in her mouth, her body yielding under me as I find her clit with my fingers

PARKER GREY

and slide them along it, spreading her juices from her lips to her nub and back again. I almost can't *believe* that I'm here, finally doing this.

I'm *finally* going to claim my princess.

I stand, taking my pants off, and Josephine doesn't move. She stays splayed on the bed, hands over her head, beautiful pussy on full display.

Mine.

I kneel on the bed between her legs, and she wraps them around me again, squeezing me with her thighs. I lean over and take one perfect, sweet nipple between my teeth and flick my tongue over the pebbled surface as she arches her back with pleasure

"Beg me," I say, my voice low and rough.

The head of my cock bumps against her entrance, parting her lips, my hand at the root guiding it.

"Please, Leo," she whispers.

I bite harder, eliciting a soft moan.

"Please what?"

"Please fuck me," she whispers, rocking her hips back and forth. I can feel the entrance of her pussy clench and spasm, like she's trying to draw me in, but I resist for another second.

"I *need* to feel you inside me," she goes on, her face hazy with lust. "Please."

I'm *never* going to get tired of hearing her say that.

"Relax, princess," I whisper. "This might hurt a little."

Josephine just watches me, her face filled with love, trust, and *lust*, and I take a deep breath.

Then I stop resisting, and let the head of my cock slide between her lips.

Chapter Fifteen

Josephine

I take a deep breath and *force* myself to relax, even though it's hard because I *want* to clench my thighs around Leo and push him inside me, *finally* feel him fill me up like I've longed for.

But I'm not dumb. I know he's *huge* down there, totally massive, and no matter how many times his fingers and tongue have been inside me, his cock is something else entirely.

"This might hurt a little," he says, and I swallow, letting my eyes drift closed.

Then the thick head of his cock slides between my lips, up to my entrance, and for the very first time, my husband *enters* me, and I gasp.

It's a sensation totally unlike *anything* else, and it's all I can think about, all I can *feel.* There's a quick twinge of pain, but it's over in a second, Leo stretching me wide.

He stops, leaning over me, just the head of his cock inside me but I'm panting for breath, bound wrists over my head.

"Are you all right?" he whispers. "You're so fucking tight, Princess."

I can't even form words, so I just nod. He kisses my cheek gently, the gesture surprisingly sweet, and then sinks in further.

I *moan*. It doesn't hurt any more — it only hurt a little, for a second — but it's completely new feeling, my pussy being filled and stretched like this, and *God* I think I like it.

Leo goes slowly, entering me millimeter by millimeter, watching my face, stroking my body. I can tell he wants *more*, wants to sheath himself balls-deep inside me, but right now he's being gentle and patient.

Nothing like the beast I once feared.

Finally, he's all the way inside me, his hips flush against mine, and the feeling of being *filled* like this, of no longer being a virgin, is wonderful and intoxicating. I feel like I can't even move, like anything I do will just make my body explode and fly into a million different pieces.

Leo's got this look of intense, total concentration on his face, like he's overwhelmed and trying not to come.

"You feel so good," I whisper, my eyes closed.

"You fit me like you were *made* for me," he growls, his lips close to my ear. "And you're so fucking tight and wet it's all I can do not to come inside you right now."

Then Leo shifts his weight, leaning on one elbow, and he lets his hand drift down my body, from my shoulders to my nipples to the down patchy right between my legs.

After a moment, his fingers find my clit, and he starts stroking me.

Instantly, sparks shoot upward through my body. I can feel my pussy clench, and Leo *growls* again, but he still doesn't move inside me, just strokes my clit faster and faster, letting his fingers do the work.

It takes seconds, because I'm already flying high, close to the edge, and all it takes is *this* and I'm crashing over, coming hard with Leo's cock deep in me. He sucks in a hard breath as I come, the shockwaves of pleasure magnified a hundredfold and I cry out his name, utterly unable to think of *anything* else.

I'm still coming, my body trembling, when he starts moving, bit by bit, but instantly it's like an electric current and I moan again, hands clenching above my binds, and he swallows hard.

"You like that, too," he whispers, still obviously trying to control himself.

"I just like it when you fuck me," I whimper, and I see a flash of the wild animal in his eyes as he pulls my legs around him, his fingers digging into my thigh as he does.

With each thrust he pulls out more and then sinks in deeper, every stroke of his thick cock still filling me completely, hitting the sensitive walls of my pussy and making me *moan*, gasp, and whimper. Leo's shaking, his hands grabbing me so hard he might leave bruises, but he's being so *gentle* right now I almost can't believe it.

I knew he would *never* hurt me, but I hadn't

realized before how *tender* he could be.

Even though he's going slow, I can feel myself building toward a climax again, and I can hear myself whisper his name, over and and over.

"Come for me again," he says, his voice a rough whisper. "I *need* to feel you come one more time."

"Leo," I whisper.

"I love you," he whispers back, and I *shatter*.

It's incredible. It's beyond incredible, I feel like I'm either flying or falling, my body filled with pure ecstasy as my vision goes totally white, my whole body tensing and jolting with the force of it.

I come *hard*, for a long time, as wave after wave rocks through me. Leo groans into my ear, his cock throbbing as he thrusts, still gentle and careful.

"I'm gonna come inside you, Princess," he whispers, and I can't even react before his cock jolts and he explodes, filling me with burst after burst.

When he finishes, he rests his forehead on mine, then kisses me gently as he takes his belt off my wrists and rubs them.

"Did you like that?" he asks, tracing my jaw with his fingers, still inside me.

"Yes," I say.

"I didn't hurt you, did I?"

I can't help but smile.

"Not at all."

He kisses me again, this kiss a little fiercer, a little rougher.

"Good," he says. "You know I'd never hurt you, don't you?"

I bite his lip gently, and he chuckles.

"Only if I ask for it," I tease.

"I wanted your first time to be gentle," he says, his voice getting lower, developing a growl. "But that doesn't mean I won't bend you over and fuck you hard like the filthy princess you are."

I swallow hard, heat stirring in me again.

"Promise?" I ask, and we kiss again.

We don't sleep that night.

Chapter Sixteen

Leo

"You did WHAT?" King Edward roars.

I squeeze Josephine's hand.

"We got married," I say.

"Without my approval?" he goes on, pacing back and forth across the sitting room. "You didn't tell us, didn't ask our advice, you just *eloped*? Just like that?"

I open my mouth to respond, but Josephine cuts me off.

"Daddy, I'm sorry we didn't tell you," she says.

"The fact that you didn't tell me is the *least* of my concerns, young lady," he says, turning sharply and pacing in the other direction. "You're a *princess*, and with your life of great wealth and leisure comes certain responsibilities, to your country and to your people."

"We were engaged anyway," she says, her voice surprisingly steady. "And I love him."

The king exhales hard, and I'm surprised fire doesn't shoot from his nostrils. The queen is sitting in a chair, watching us quietly, thinking.

"There are *protocols* surrounding this sort of thing," he goes on. "You can't just *go get married* on a whim, Josephine. What's that going to look like to the public? I'll tell you, it looks like we've got a daughter who makes rash decisions, who's mercurial and tempestuous, who doesn't even tell *her own family* when she decides to get married..."

"Jo," her mother says quietly. "We wish you'd told us."

Suddenly Josephine squeezes my hand even harder, and her mom's words hit me like a punch to the gut.

I hadn't even *thought* of that. My own parents have been distant at best since Nadia died, so it just didn't occur to me that Josephine's parents would be this upset and not seeing their daughter get married.

But of course they are, and I feel awful.

Josephine's mouth opens slightly, she swallows hard.

"I'm sorry," she says, still squeezing my hand like her life depends on it. "I didn't think..."

"That's right," her father says, entering the conversation again. "You *didn't* think."

"Edward," the queen says, and the king stops pacing and looks up at her. She puts out one hand, palm outward, in the universal *calm down* gesture.

He stops pacing.

"Prince Leo, would you be so good as to give us a moment alone with Josephine?" she asks.

I don't want to. I know they're her parents, and they're clearly not going to harm her, but I don't like the thought of leaving her alone, without me for backup.

But I look down at her, and she nods.

"Please, it's fine," she says.

"You're sure?"

"Of course."

I don't like it, but I'll obey my princess.

I bow to the room and leave.

• • •

Josephine's in there for a long time, and though there are raised voices once or twice, for the most part they talk quietly and I can't hear what they're saying.

That doesn't mean I leave. I sit on a bench in the hall outside the room, just *waiting* in case my princess needs me. Last night I swore to never leave her side, and even though a conversation with her parents wasn't exactly what I had in mind, this is as good a place to start as any.

Finally, the heavy door cracks open. I practically leap to my feet, afraid that Josephine's going to come out and leap into my arms, crying hysterically.

I'm afraid that somehow, her father has the power to annul our marriage, even though I *know* he doesn't.

But Josephine is smiling, even though I can tell she's been crying, and I pull her into my arms.

"I'm fine," she says.

"You were crying."

"Yeah, well..." she says, her voice drifting off. "I

didn't mean to, but I hurt their feelings."

She takes a deep breath and pulls away from me, looking me in the eye.

"What do you think about getting married again next week?" she asks.

I kiss her, once on the lips, and once on each tear-stained cheek.

"I'd marry you every week," I say.

• • •

A few days later, we have an engagement banquet, followed by an engagement ball. I know there are rumors floating around about *why* we're getting married so soon after announcing the engagement, but I make up something about my parents wanting a daughter-in-law soon, and I also, I don't give a shit about the rumors.

At both events, I can hardly keep my hands off of Josephine. It's all I can do not to *shout* from the rafters that she's mine, already my bride, and that I'm *hers* for forever. We hold hands under the banquet table, and it's all I can do not to slide my hand into her lap, lift the long skirt of her gown, and tease her until she comes right there, in the middle of everything.

Afterward, I'm impossibly hard for the entire ball, just *watching* her glide around the floor, beautiful and graceful as a swan. She dances with everyone there — it's only polite, after all — and even though all the other men are perfectly courteous and well-mannered, by the end of it I'm responding to my own dance partner with one-word answers, watching Josephine from the corner of my eye.

It's not that I don't trust her. It's not that I feel like there's any real *threat* from any of these men.

I just don't want to fucking watch anyone else dance with my princess, and it works me into a near-frenzy of possessiveness.

Finally, I can't stand it any more. There's a lull in the dancing while the band takes a break, and I find Josephine, talking to her two sisters and a few other people.

I smile as charmingly as I *possibly* can, though I still see nervousness flicker over a few of the faces.

"Ladies," I say, winding my hand through

Josephine's. "Could I steal my fiancée away for a few moments?"

They all agree, giggling a little, and I lead Josephine through the dance hall, to an outside door, and we emerge into the cool night air.

"What is—"

I lean down and kiss her, because I feel like if I don't kiss her *right now*, I might dissolve. Josephine practically melts under my lips, her soft body yielding instantly, and a surge of heat spikes through me.

My hands lock around her waist, and her fingers wind through my hair. I kiss her greedily, urgently, our bodies pressing together as I invade her mouth with my tongue, *possessing* her.

"I need you *now*," I growl when we separate.

She looks around nervously. We're outside in a balustrade, not far from the lit windows of the dance hall where *everyone* we know is still standing.

"Leo, it's—"

I kiss her again, and this time I slide both hands down to her ass, squeezing her firm cheeks hard and rocking her body against my massive, insistent erection. I can practically feel her heartbeat fluttering in her chest, and I break the kiss to whisper into her ear.

"I want to fuck you so hard you forget your own name," I murmur. "You're so fucking beautiful that I can't stand it."

Josephine bites her lip, her eyes lowering. Even though I've been talking to her like this for weeks now, she blushes, but it only makes me harder.

"Okay," she whispers, and grabs my hand. "Come on."

I let her pull me along until we're at a doorway. Josephine tries the handle, but it's locked.

"Shit," she mutters, and pulls her hand out of mine.

I swallow hard, leaning against the wall, hoping that no one comes along and sees us breaking into a locked room in the palace. Not that I care, but I'm *trying* to get along with my future in-laws. For my princess' sake.

She lifts the handle, twists it slightly, makes a face, and then suddenly the door swings open and Josephine grins.

"We figured that out as kids," she says, and *winks* at me.

We're through the door in a flash, and I push it shut behind us. It's some kind of store room, but the kind of store room you could only find at a palace — there are some boxes and furniture, but also a suit of armor, a huge painting of a forbidding-looking woman, and a corner filled with rolled-up rugs.

I grab Josephine's hand and yanking her back against me, her body warm and supple, and she arches into me, turning her head for another kiss, slowly grinding her perfect ass against my erection.

I groan from somewhere deep in my chest, and Josephine bites my lip, already panting for breath.

This isn't going to be slow and romantic, this is going to be quick and rough and *hard*. I reach down her top and find her nipples already hard as diamonds, and I pinch one as she moans into my mouth.

That's *all* it takes.

I push Josephine forward until she's pinned against a big wooden crate, probably holding priceless jewels or something. I don't know, and I don't care as I move my hands up her back, pushing her forward as I grind my still-clothed cock against her heat and she looks over her shoulder, eyes heavy-lidded with lust.

"Say it," I command.

"I need you to fuck me," she says, her voice as soft and submissive as always, still sounding innocent and girlish even though she knows *exactly* what she's doing to me.

I run one thumb down the cleft between her cheeks, lingering on the tight bud of her asshole for just a moment, and even through the fabric of her gown I can feel her shudder with desire. I still haven't claimed her ass, no matter how badly I want to — it takes time and preparation, and when I finally do I want my princess to *love* having my cock there.

Then I keep going, to her lips so swollen with desire that I can feel them through her skirt, to her clit.

God, I can't take this. I lift her skirt with one hand and unbutton and unzip my pants with the other. When her gown is around her hips, I grin in surprise.

She's soaking wet, and not wearing panties. I

pause for a moment, stroking my cock with one hand and her slippery entrance with the other.

"You planned for this," I say, my voice gravelly.

"I had a feeling," she says, looking back at me, that mixture of submission and seduction in her eyes.

I grab her hair and push her down *just* hard enough that it doesn't hurt, and she gasps with pleasure and anticipation.

Then I take her with a single thrust, sheathing myself in her as she sighs, her eyes rolling back into her head. She's every bit as tight as she was the first time I took her, but in the days since we've fucked every which way and I *know* she can take my cock like this.

"Is this why you didn't wear panties?" I ask, pulling out and then bottoming out in her again. This time she gasps and moans, because I *know* my cock is hitting every sweet pleasure spot inside her.

"Yes," Josephine gasps. "God, fuck yes."

"And you *like* getting bent over a box in a store room and fucked hard," I say, thrusting faster, harder. "That's not very polite of you, Princess."

"Fuck polite," she gasps. "Make me come, Leo."

I fuck her even harder, my hips slamming into hers, and Josephine moans and whimpers. The entire palace guard could kick in this door right now and there's no *way* I would stop.

This, right here — Josephine bent over in front me, my cock filling her completely as she moans, making her come while I'm in total control — this is *everything*.

Her muscles start fluttering around me, and I can tell she's about to come, but I want something *more*. Something *else*, because I'm addicted and obsessed with her, and because I love that even here, now, where we could be found any minute, her body is *mine* and I can do anything I want.

I pull out. She turns her head, baffled and confused, but I keep my grip on her with one hand and dip three fingers inside her with the other, getting them slippery and sticky with her juices.

Then I slide them up, from her seam to her back hole, circling it with my fingers.

Josephine bites her lip and closes her eyes, her body softening under mine. This isn't the first time I've done this, and I know that even though she thinks it's *filthy*, she loves it.

I slide one finger into her ass, feeling her clench. I wait for her to relax, then I slide in a second finger, waiting again.

This time she flexes her hips against my hand, like she's asking for more, so I slowly, carefully add the third one.

"You like it when I fill your ass, Princess?" I whisper.

Gently, carefully, I move my fingers inside her tight back hole, feeling her respond, pushing back against me.

"Yes," she says.

"You're so fucking dirty," I murmur. "And I love you for it."

I take my hand off her hair, grabbing my cock again. When I push it against her entrance she gasps and tenses, but I don't stop, and after a moment she relaxes.

I ease myself into her, incredibly, *impossibly* tight, and Josephine practically melts.

"Leo," she whimpers. "Oh, *fuck*, Leo, that feels so fucking *good*..."

I almost come on the spot, and I know I can't last long, not like *this*. It's not just that I'm filling both her holes at once. I'm doing it *here*, and she's letting me.

I could fuck her *anywhere* I wanted, any *way* I wanted, and that's the sexiest fucking thing I can think of.

In seconds I'm fucking her hard again and Josephine is moaning, babbling a combination of my name and the word *fuck* over and over until she comes so hard she buries her face in her elbow, her pussy and ass clenching around me like a vise.

I only last one more stroke before I come too, unloading myself deep inside her, pure pleasure and satisfaction rocketing through me in a surge so strong it nearly knocks me over.

It takes us a long time to catch our breath, but when we do, I take my fingers out of her ass, then pull her upright. I'm still inside her, but she arches her back and turns to kiss me, long and slow and lingering.

"I love you," she whispers.

"I love you more," I say.

We kiss again, and I have an idea.

"I'm going to claim your ass on our second wedding night," I murmur, and I feel her pussy clench around me.

"That's in a few days," she murmurs.

"I *need* you," I say. "And I want to possess every *inch* of you. I want to make you feel pleasure you didn't think was possible."

She smiles a little.

"You do," she says.

Chapter Seventeen

Josephine

The next few days pass in a blur. Under *no* circumstances are we to tell anyone that we're already married, and even though a few very blurry pictures *alleged* to be the two of us in Montblanche surface, those are easy enough to deny.

We're *already* getting married, why would we have eloped?

But every night, Leo comes and sleeps in my bed. Well, we don't sleep, at least not at first, though after a few rounds we usually drift off, his arms around me.

Waking up next to him is the *best*.

• • •

"Hurry *up*," I say, impatient. The ceremony was supposed to start fifteen minutes ago, and even though no one expects a wedding to be on a time, I'd at least like to get fake-married *today*.

And then I'd like to get past the dinner and the dancing to *tonight*, to what Leo's promised me every night since he took me in the castle store room.

I'm nervous, but I'm *excited* and dear God am I aroused at the thought. I know I probably shouldn't be, because butts are pretty gross, but when Leo puts his fingers there?

Or when he puts his *tongue* there? It feels *mind-blowingly* good, even moreso because it's the sort of thing that nice, innocent princesses aren't supposed to do.

"This would go faster if you hadn't picked the dress with ten thousand buttons," Katarina responds, still fiddling with the closure.

I feel *slightly* bad for wearing a white wedding dress and not being a virgin, but I'm also pretty sure it doesn't matter. I'm also *pretty* sure that virtually no one in the modern world is still a virgin when they get married — except me, of course, but that was...

different.

"It's a nice dress," I say. "And it was the royal seal of approval."

Katarina just snorts. The royal seal of approval is pretty tough, and this dress only got it because it's got a lace overlay that's long-sleeve, making it appropriately modest for a Tomassian wedding.

Poor Katarina, who somehow talked our parents into letting her marry two men at the same time, practically had to wear a nun's habit.

"Okay," she finally says, stepping away. She's got one hand on her enormous belly as she surveys me. "You're just about ready to go. Where's your bouquet?"

"Here," volunteers Florentina, who was sitting quietly on a chair this whole time, just *watching*.

"Thanks," I say.

"You look nice," Florentina says softly.

"You do too," I tell them both, dressed in matching blue dresses. "Ready to go get me married?"

• • •

Even though this isn't our *real* wedding ceremony, it somehow feels that way. Not that the first one didn't — but they feel *different*, and I'm glad I'm doing this one, marrying Leo in front of both our families and our kingdoms.

Maybe *now* the rumors will finally stop. I don't think that *everyone* will stop seeing him as a beast, but maybe having a queen and children will help his image out some.

After the ceremony, we eat a huge banquet, though I'm too excited and nervous to eat more than a few bites. Now that the wedding part is over, I'm wet as *hell* with anticipation of what comes next.

Then we dance. It's only *polite* that I dance with most of the men in attendance, even though the only one I really want to dance with is my new husband. Every time we lock eyes on the dance floor he gives me a long, slow, *burning* look that just about lights me on fire.

At last, at *last*, the dance ends. The band plays us out, and there's a horse and carriage to take us to a secluded cabin on the palace grounds — our person

RULE ME DIRTY

honeymoon suite.

When we arrive, Leo steps out, then holds his hand out for me.

"Princess," he says, smiling, and I take his hand.

Before I'm out of the carriage he's lifting me in his arms, and as the carriage drives off he pushes open the cottage door, carrying me across the threshold, and he kicks it shut behind him before carrying me straight to the bedroom and putting me down on the bed.

Even though it's a cabin, it's still a *royal* cabin, with antique furniture that's probably a hundred years old at least, everything sumptuous, outfitted in velvet and silk. The bed is an enormous four-poster bed, the posts reaching for the ceiling, all the furniture beautifully finished and hand-carved.

Also, there's a huge mirror in a gilded frame, pointed *directly* at the bed.

Instantly, he's on me, crushing my mouth with his, hungrily devouring me. I grab at his jacket and shirt, wanting to get them off of his perfect, chiseled body already, but he pushes my hands away.

"We do things *my* way tonight, Princess," he says,

and pushes the skirt of my wedding dress over my hips.

I *did* wear panties today, because it seemed too risky not to, but in half a second he's torn my thong off my body and his tongue is on my lips, sliding between them and lapping at my clit.

Heat rockets through me, and I moan. There's something *especially* urgent about Leo right now, like he's got some deep, unnameable hunger that *demands* to be satisfied.

He licks harder, lapping and sucking at my clit and I moan helplessly, turning my face toward the sheets on the bed. Leo's always been fucking *amazing* with his tongue, but now that he's been practicing on me I swear he can make me come in a matter of seconds.

Then his fingers part my lips and *plunge* inside me, stroking my sensitive inner wall, and I come almost instantly.

Leo doesn't wait for me to finish, and I'm still trembling as he flips me over onto my hands and knees, pulling me toward him and he pushes his fingers back inside me. His tongue moves from my clit upward, and I hold my breath in anticipation of what's coming.

Slowly, he licks me *there*, and I exhale in a rush, still gripping the bedsheets tight. It's so *dirty*, so *wrong*, but it feels so *good* as he coaxes me to another orgasm, tongue lavishing attention on my puckered back hole.

This time I whimper his name when I come, and when I'm finished, aftershocks still rattling through me, he crawls over me and kisses the back of my neck.

"I love how dirty you are," he says, something he tells me every night. "You're fucking perfect."

He kisses my neck slowly.

"And I'm going to fuck you in the ass tonight, Princess," he goes on, sending a shiver down my spine. "But I'm going to make you come every way I know how first."

Leo slides his hands down my back, gently, *seductively*, and then stops midway.

Suddenly he grabs the fabric and *pulls*. The dress tears and tiny buttons go flying all over the room, and I gasp in shock, but it's so fucking *hot* that I don't mind.

He keeps going, *tearing* my wedding dress with his bare hands, ripping the white fabric apart until he tosses it away and pulls me backward against his body, tearing my bra away until I'm naked and he's fully clothed.

We're facing the mirror, and he's looking over my shoulder, his hands all over me. I've never watched myself like this before, but it's *sexy*, seeing what he's doing to me.

And thinking about what he's *going* to do.

Leo kneels on the bed and pulls me onto his lap, holding tightly onto my hips so I don't slide off. The massive spike of his erection is right underneath me, and I can't help but writhe against, rubbing him against my most sensitive spots.

"Fuck, you're sexy," he says into my ear, one hand wandering up to pinch a nipple. "Do you like watching yourself, Princess?"

"I do now," I murmur.

"Good," he says. "Because you're going to watch yourself take my cock."

He lets me go, pulling his shirt off before tilting

me forward onto my hands and knees. In a flash, he's naked as well, thick erection jutting out proudly, and he kneels again on the bed behind me.

I bite my lip, *waiting*. Anticipating that sweet, *glorious* moment when he slides into me, that moment when the world starts exploding.

But instead he pulls me back so I'm kneeling over him, both of us facing the mirror, my legs straddling his. He shifts slightly, his hands on my hips, and then, *finally*, he's at my entrance.

"Fuck me, Princess," he growls, and pulls me back onto his cock.

I gasp and moan, nearly going off balance, but Leo's strong hands hold me upright.

"Leo," I sigh, pleasure fizzing through my body the way it always does. In moments he's sunk completely inside me, filling me up and hitting every single spot inside me, and I bite my lip, rocking back and forth.

It feels *good*, like I never want to stop even after I come again and again.

"Open your eyes," he murmurs, and I obey, looking at the mirror, and suddenly, there we are.

Leo's hands are roaming all over my body, and I'm moving slowly, my breasts bouncing a little as I watch him disappear inside me.

I've never watched myself like this before, and it's... *hot*.

Leo's hands tighten on me, and before I know it I'm moving up and down on his cock, watching him fill me completely with every stroke. It's intoxicating, and even though I've already come twice, I can feel the wave building inside me, threatening to burst free.

"I love watching you fuck me," Leo says. "Almost as much as I love feeling you come when I'm inside you."

I can't stop watching, because it's hypnotic and *beyond* sexy, and I come with both eyes open, Leo watching me over my own shoulder. Just as I climax he pulls me down onto him hard, going as deep as he *possibly* can, letting me jolt and writhe against him with his face against my ear.

"That feels so *good*," I whimper. I'm still rolling my hips, moving him inside me just a little. "Leo, I come so hard when you're inside me."

Leo kisses my cheek gently, but then he wraps one arm around my waist and pitches me forward, onto my hands and knees, cock still buried deep. I gasp at the impact, toes curling, and he grabs a pillow, shoving it under my hips.

And then he *fucks* me like he can't take it any more, as hard as he ever has. In seconds I'm on my elbows, ass high in the air as he plows into me, mercilessly, again and again, his enormous cock going deep with every stroke and hitting every *single* spot inside my channel.

All I can do is moan, and I think I'm moaning his name but I don't even know. I don't want him to stop, I just want him to keep going, hard and fast and so so *good*.

I come again, all the muscles in my body shaking and trembling, and I swear to God I *scream* his name into the pillow under my face. It's the only word I can think, let *alone* say.

As it ends, Leo pulls out. I take a deep breath and look up, about to beg him not to stop, but he's reaching over me and to the bedside table, where he pulls out a clear bottle.

My eyes go wide, and he leans over me, kissing me roughly. I'm prone, completely vulnerable, utterly submissive right now but I still *want* this. I want him all night, then all day, and into forever.

"You didn't forget, did you?" he murmurs.

The top clicks off the bottle, and I can hear him squeezing something.

"No," I whisper.

Leo slides one finger between my buttocks, the length of my cleft, and *right* onto my puckered back hole.

I gasp as he stokes me gently, then pushes it in, slowly, and the sensation's like *nothing* else, a little strange but good in a way that sends shivers over my whole body.

"Don't stop," I moan.

Leo slides a second finger into my ass, and I grab the sheets in a handful. Moments later his cock is at my entrance again, and he slides into me and I cry out, filled in both holes.

It feels so good I can't even *think*, just make noise as he fucks me slowly, carefully, then slides in a third finger.

I come again. It's fucking uncontrollable, almost *embarrassing* how he has this level of control over my body, but I don't care. As long as he's doing *this*, I don't care.

He pulls out. I'm panting for breath and pretty sure I couldn't move right now if my life depended on it, but I still want more. I want more until I can't come any more.

I want to give him *everything* I have, give him every part of my body. Make him feel half as good as he makes me.

"Relax," Leo murmurs, and then the tip of his cock is at my back entrance.

Chapter Eighteen

Leo

God, she's fucking beautiful, on her hands and knees in front of me, still trembling from her last orgasm, looking at me over her shoulder like she *still* wants more, like she can't get enough.

And she's mine. *All* mine, totally and utterly my princess.

I guide the tip of my cock to her back entrance and swallow hard, because I'm still afraid of hurting her. But I want her, every *part* of her.

And I want Josephine to feel every kind of pleasure imaginable.

I ease the tip of my cock in, watching, transfixed, as it disappears into her ass. Josephine sighs softly as I slide in, bit by bit, going so slow it's excruciating because she's so tight it's like a fist around my cock.

Only tighter.

When I finally pop the head of my cock into her, Josephine gasps. I have to stop for a minute, afraid that I'm going to come, and I stroke her back as she takes a deep breath.

"Don't stop," she whispers, her voice shaky. "Please don't stop."

Jesus, there's never been a more perfect girl in the whole world.

"Does it feel good to have my cock in your ass?" I murmur.

Josephine just swallows and nods.

I ease myself into her little by little, as slowly as I possibly can until I'm completely inside her. It's fucking unbelievable, how good this feels, and I know I can't last very long.

"Your ass feels fucking incredible, princess," I whisper.

She doesn't answer, just *moans*, her breath coming in sharp pants.

I force myself to go slowly, *gently*, but it doesn't matter. Josephine is grunting and shouting with every stroke of my thick cock, animal noises of pure ecstasy.

Just as I think I can't possibly hold out any longer, she comes, every muscle clenching and squeezing me so tightly my vision turns white as she moans into the pillow.

I empty myself into her, every last drop, and I keep going until I can tell she's completely finished and exhausted, so I pull out and then gather her into my arms, kissing her deeply.

"You're incredible and I love you," I whisper. "And I promise to love you forever, just like this."

She smiles, her face hazy.

"I love you too," she whispers. "I'm glad we got married twice."

I kiss her again, and when we wake up the next morning, we're in the exact same position.

. . .

A few days after our second wedding, Josephine and I move to Szegravia, where I've got duties to fulfill as the Crown Prince. Even though it's different from what she's used to, Josephine's presence in the dark, forbidding palace makes the whole place feel lighter, airier, more *spirited*.

My parents like her at first, but slowly, they grow to love her. No one will ever replace my sister Nadia, of course, but Josephine slowly becomes like a daughter to them.

And the people of Szegravia *love* their new crown princess, rumors about an elopement aside. They even love her so much that they all seem to forget all the horrible things they said about me for years and years.

Our lives together are nearly perfect. She brings the sunshine back to my life, and I'd do *anything* to make her happy.

I didn't believe in fairy tales before, but I think I do now.

Epilogue

Josephine

Four Years Later

Next to the couch, the baby monitor squawks, and I sigh. Leo stops massaging my feet to pause the movie we were watching, and we look at each other.

"Your turn," I say.

"It was my turn last time," he says, lifting one eyebrow.

I just put one hand on my huge, eight-months-pregnant belly, and lift an eyebrow back at him.

"Do you have a crane to get me off the couch?" I ask.

Leo stands, leans over to kiss me, and then disappears upstairs. I shift on the couch, trying to find a more comfortable position, but I don't think there *is* one any more.

As if in protest, my daughter kicks me right in the ribcage, and I take a deep breath, tilting my head back against the couch.

On the baby monitor, I can hear Leo soothing our nearly-two-year old, George. Our oldest, Henry, is nearly four, and *he* sleeps like a champion. George usually does too, though right now he's going through a phase where he wakes up every hour and wants a glass of water or something.

Our daughter kicks again, and I put one hand on my belly, in the vague hope that it'll soothe her or something. She's already feistier than either of the boys was, and as much as I love being pregnant — and as much as Leo loves me being pregnant — I can't wait until she's actually here.

He's a good dad. That didn't surprise me, but I *was* surprised at how excited he was. It was only a few months after we got married, and to be honest, I'd barely given birth control a second thought — I figured we'd have to actually start *trying* or something before I got pregnant.

Nope. But Leo was ecstatic, so happy he almost

cried. I knew he wanted kids, but I didn't know he wanted them *that* badly.

And as my belly swelled... well, kids weren't the *only* thing he wanted. If I thought he was insatiable before, that was *nothing* compared to Leo when I'm pregnant. We once got caught fucking in the pantry of his parents' kitchen because he *just* couldn't control himself.

This baby is the last one, though the sex has made me think that we *could* have one more.

Finally, Leo comes back down the stairs.

"He down?" I ask, keeping my voice low.

"He's down," Leo confirms, sitting back on the couch. He hits the play button on the movie again, but instead of watching it, he leans over and kisses my belly.

"How are my girls?" he asks, running a hand over the taut skin.

I guide his palm to the last place she kicked, and he waits. Nothing. I sigh.

"Of course," I say. "She was kicking up a storm a second ago."

He kisses me again, then sits up, pulling me onto

his lap.

"I think we've got at least half an hour before George wakes up again," he says, his hand snaking between my thighs. "We could watch this movie, or..."

"Or we could fuck on the couch?" I offer, grinning.

"My thoughts exactly," he says.

He kisses me, gently at first but then harder, and soon we're not paying any attention to the movie because I'm doing my best not to moan as Leo enters me from behind, the only position we can still use right now.

Afterward, we lie naked and sweaty on the couch. Almost exactly on time, there's another little voice from the baby monitor, and Leo stands up, pulling on his pants.

"I'll go," he says.

"I love you," I say, as he drops a kiss on my forehead.

"I love you too," he says, and walks up the stairs to comfort our son for the fourth time that night.

ABOUT PARKER GREY

I write obsessed, dominant, alpha heroes who stop at *nothing* to get their women - and get them dirty!

I can be found driving around my small, southern town in either my minivan or hubby's pickup truck. No one here is the wiser about my secret writing life… and I definitely prefer it that way!